# WILD THINGS

## A ROMANCE NOVEL

RITIKA KOCHHAR

Made with ♥ on the Notion Press Platform
www.notionpress.com

To the strong women in my family.

# Contents

# Foreword

This book is a work of fiction. Any similarity to actual persons, living or dead, or actual events, is purely coincidental."

# Acknowledgements

This short story was written because a friend challenged me to write a romance. I love romances, especially Susan Elizabeth Phillips, Judith Mcnaught, and Jane Feather. I even love the romances written by Sir Terry Pratchett - because they're about strong men and women and relationships that encapsulate entire families. So, that's what I've written.

Sid, Raghu, Richa - thank you always. You keep me writing with your can-do attitudes.

Rita & Sonali - You keep me going, period!

# CHAPTER ONE

"Do you have endless nights?"

The voice was deep and male. Raqia kept her head studiously bent over her computer, but she couldn't prevent the snort of laughter that she managed to swallow just in time. 'A man asking for a title like that? I wonder if he's buying romance novels for his wife or daughter. On second thoughts, with that name, it's definitely for his wife', she thought wryly. 'I know Dehradun's filled with readers with all kinds of preferences, but a man openly admitting to reading romances is still going to raise a few eyebrows...'

"Who's it by, sir", Mayank, her younger brother asked from behind the counter. "I can look it up on the computer. But romances are all in that corner there". She squeezed her eyes shut to keep from laughing out loud, or getting up to help them both. It was Mayank's shop really, not hers. After all, he was the one who lived here through the week. And he was usually very polite with customers, even though, right now she could hear the smirk in his voice.

There was silence for a minute before a deep guffaw of laughter broke out behind her. She reluctantly raised her head again. 'Let Mayank deal with customers. He's a good salesperson', she reminded herself. 'But I'm older. It's up to me to help them out,' her inner voice argued back. She took a deep breath and her second thoughts kicked in. 'I do not have the time for this today,' it said in a voice that resounded firmly in her head.

"Will I find weirdoes from another planet or something under the bed is drooling there as well", the voice asked in an amused tone.

She raised her eyes heavenward before resignedly closing the top of her computer. 'Just a few more minutes to finish this. Was that too much to ask', she grumbled to whoever it was who listened up there. 'And especially if I have to deal with weirdoes from another planet'. She sighed again. 'Almost an MA from Oxford and here I am running after two siblings and a father who doesn't feel like a father and trying to micromanage a bookshop in Dehradun while I work AND hold classes. What am I doing? When is it going to be my time? Ooooh shit, what IS the time', she hurriedly looked up at the clock and gulped. "Oh, my God, Oh, my God. Forty minutes left", she murmured out loud before speeding up her typing. The three interesting hours of her life right now were the class she taught to the cadets at the Military Academy in Dehradun. Granted, all of them thought they were better at urban warfare than her and had no time for her lessons on the Middle East, but it still gave her a thrill to teach and it was nice of her boss to organize it. It also gave her time in Bade Papaji's bookshop which had been her home from the moment her father left. More importantly, it was just so great to get away from the boring program work in Delhi and her life as her father's caretaker. 'I think of Dehradun as a holiday. That's how desperate I am,' she groused to herself.

She heaved a third deep sigh as she reopened the tab for Arab News on her laptop. The Middle East and urban warfare may have been the topic of her thesis back when she'd been at Oxford but that had been more than ten years ago. But it was the reason her boss, DD had asked her to give the lectures. She had been so happy to get away from Delhi that she'd agreed and now she needed to include information about the current situation in the lectures to make them relevant. This meant she had to summarise Middle Eastern politics and personalities. 'What was I thinking? I could have said that there are way too many countries under that term. I could have said that it was a topic that required a Ph.D. Instead, I just agreed to sum up years and years of studies into two weeks of three-hour lectures each. Raqia, you need to stand up for yourself. This is crazy. This is the toughest thing I've ever done and I've done some tough things in my time.'

'No', she revised that. 'The toughest part of her lectures was that bugger, Aggarwal. The CO of the research institute was horrible. He may have been a Kargil war hero but he was a creep. Constantly trying to touch her while trying to belittle her brains. She didn't know which part of her she was supposed to protect first? Her brains or her boobs when he stared at them while making belittling comments.

"Beta, shouldn't you be eating lunch", the Major's deep voice spoke from the top of the stairs. "Isn't it getting late? You need to eat something".

"Five minutes, Dad", Raqia almost snarled as she tapped furiously. 'Was her family never going to leave her alone? She'd finally got the twins to finish college...well, one of them at least, and now the Major was back and she had to take care of him. She was never going to get away. This was going to be her life forever. She paused and took a deep breath. 'Oh God, what am I saying', she thought remorsefully. 'I'm so lucky. Badi Amma and Papaji were there for the boys and me throughout our growing-up years.

A memory of the last phone call they'd received before the Major vanished flashed through her mind. "Raqia", he'd said in Punjabi, trying to speak over the market sounds in the background. "It's going to take me some time to get back. You will have to look after the boys for me. They will also ask you to vacate the house in NDA. Ask your grandmother to help you clean up the place. Tell her you'll be staying with her a little longer". She still winced when she remembered that nightmarish conversation. Cleaning out the house in the cantonment; calling their bewildered grandparents and telling them papa wasn't coming back just yet and the three of them would be staying with them; getting the boys and her discharged from school in Pune. She'd been fourteen. Thank God for Raman and Sudeep uncles. They and their wives had helped every minute of the way.

'I managed,' she thought stoutly. 'I was fourteen and I managed. It took him twenty-three years to return but he did. So, what if he's a bit different now. We expected that.'

'But he's a different man from my funny and gorgeous and affectionate dad. He's nothing like what I remember,' her second thoughts wailed as memories of her father flooded through her brain – throwing her into the air when he returned from office; lying with her head on his shoulder while he read aloud from "*Where The Wild Things Are*" and '*A Wrinkle In Time*'; of standing proudly while he was saluted by young officers.

'Of course, he's a stranger,' she stoutly replied to herself. 'What do you expect? I've grown up while he was stuck in limbo all these years. Not his fault. I just have to deal with this too'.

"Hey sis", Abhay yelled cheerfully as he walked through the door. "Hi Dad", he said more respectfully as he spotted his father on the stairs.

Raqia jerked as her internal argument was rudely interrupted. She glanced at the watch on her computer to realize she'd used up her precious five minutes in her internal argument. She raised her fingers, indicating that she'd take five more minutes. "Get changed and get lunch on the table", she ordered her younger brother. "I'll be there as soon as I finish..."

"Or we can just eat Maggi", her brother said as he grinned cheerfully. "It's also a fine day for pizza. It's a holiday".

Raqia looked up and grinned back at her brother. "Well, it's not technically, but I get your point. That will give me an extra two and a half minutes with Prince Salman", she agreed. "Okay with you, dad?"

Their father stood on the stairs looking lost for a minute before he shrugged and walked down. Abhay gave a cheer as he ran around to the kitchen. She could hear him asking Kulpreet to make sandwiches, pizzas, and cold coffee. She got up and ran behind him. "Soup. It's too cold for cold coffee", she said sternly. "And lots of veggies in the Maggi".

Her brother grinned cheekily. "Aren't you running late on Prince Salman", he laughed. "Don't you want to research him a bit more? What will you tell the world about him if you don't stalk him properly? Find out who he's spending his evenings with?"

Raqia blinked. 'Wasn't there someone looking for Endless Nights? There had been a customer in the shop. He hadn't come back to the counter. Where was he?'

She turned around reluctantly. The man and Mayank were walking towards the bookcases where comics were kept now. All she could see was that he was tall – very tall, and broad. His hair was salt and pepper and the little bit of neck that she could see between the hair and sweater was dark and as thick as a small tree trunk. His hips swiveled loosely when he walked while his shoulders stayed stiffly in place – the mark of someone who lifted weights.

Raqia blinked. That walk. She'd seen it before. And the shoulders. She remembered the arms and neck being less oxlike but the walk was...

Mayank had his face turned towards the man walking beside him. The bedazzled look on his face was also suspiciously familiar. She blinked.

And groaned inwardly as she felt herself become hot inside. 'Even that little bit of connection to HIM,' she thought, 'and I became red with...embarrassment. Definitely embarrassment.'

She looked closer. That little bit of dark skin on the neck was too dark. It looked suspiciously like the end of a tattoo. The man had a tattoo on his back.

"Don't worry, yaar. You and I aren't the types to need a book to enjoy some endless nights", the man teased Mayank further. There was an immediate if reluctant smile on her brothers' face as he found himself drawn into the aura of the big man. Raqia stared suspiciously at the back in front of her and the newly sprung smile of adoration on Mayank's face. 'It couldn't be', she thought to herself in disbelief. She'd seen that look before – often on young soldiers' faces. A long time back. When her dad was teaching at NDA. The last she'd heard about Captain Varin Paranjape was that he'd caught his CO by the collar for not giving him leave to take his pregnant wife to the hospital.

She shook her head, wryly. Of course, it wasn't him. Why would that lout be here? He was more likely to be in a shady bar somewhere after a court-martial. You do not catch your CO by his collar in public. It wasn't done.

Except, the man walking towards her with a Calvin and Hobbes in his hand was Varin Paranjape. He was just a lot older. And tougher.

A bolt of lightning struck her insides, lighting up various parts of her, including her face. 'Am I tomato red or just flushing', she wondered to herself. 'Where all does he have tattoos', her second thoughts intervened.

Varin opened his mouth and Raqia tensed. Would he remember her? She raised a hand to pat down her hair. 'Thank God I'm dressed decently', she thought frantically. 'I've even got lipstick and contacts on this morning', she thought proudly. She never got it right normally. She'd caught a break today.

"Major Harkirat Singh", he inquired, looking straight at her father.

'He didn't even notice me', Raqia realized in disbelief.

Her father tensed as he looked up, a hunted look on his face. There was nowhere for him to go. "Yes", he muttered doubtfully.

"I studied under you at NDA, Sir", the big burly man said quietly. "I'm Varin Paranjape".

"I...I don't remember", her father almost whimpered. "I mean...so many boys".

Raqia winced, seeing the Major through a stranger's eye. That man Varin Paranjpe knew twenty-three years ago; her father had been adored by everyone. He'd been warm and gorgeous and strong enough to lift both the twins up at the same time. He used to throw her in the air even when she was twelve.

He was still tall but painfully thin. His hair had grown out of the short buzz cut the army had given him before sending him home four months ago and now fell greasily over the collar of his old khaki sweater. He was wearing camel-colored warm trousers that were held up with a belt. The shoes were old but still better than the rest of his clothes. They were the only part of the old wardrobe that still fit properly. His face was dark. You had to be close to see the scars but they were there. It was a far cry from the Major Varin Paranjape had known.

She closed her eyes to shut out the memories. 'The boys need to get his hair cut. And we need to find him better fitting clothes. We should have taken him shopping. I'm going to have to give up my Saturday', she thought with a frown. 'HE shouldn't have seen him looking like this. What will HE think?'

"Varin darling, yoohoo", a feminine voice trilled from the entrance. Raqia kept her eyes shut and tried to melt into the background before she remembered it was her shop and she was there to serve customers. The beloved wife Varin Paranjape had hit his CO for would be around. 'You're so dumb, Raqia', she berated herself. 'Grow up.'

"What a cute shop", the voice cooed and Raqia reluctantly opened her eyes and stood up. "Thanks", she muttered as she turned to the door. After all, the shop was cute. A friend's mother had personally supervised it via Internet from Dartmouth. More importantly, it was filled to the brim with the best books that they could bring in from all over, and the food was excellent. But it leaked money like a shipwreck.

The boys and she had worked very hard to turn their grandparent's bookshop into something they loved spending time in. It was slowly becoming popular, but not enough to make a profit. They'd done the coffee shop part to look like a fairy grotto with fairy lights, tiny fairies peeping out from various places including the murals on the walls and lots of green tablecloths. The book shop had a magic theme with wands, spells, and magical animals painted on the walls. It even had false tree stumps for people to sit on as they browsed the books.

The woman standing in front of her looked like she had been made to order to match the shop. She looked like a small fairy with white open hair, a cowboy hat, long dangling earrings, a poncho, and high boots under a long yellow and brown skirt. 'She's older than Varin Paranjape', Raqia thought, outraged.

"I can't believe we found this treasure! I'm going to come to Dehradun just to spend time here.", she cooed huskily as she looked around. She turned towards Abhay. "So, what do you recommend we eat? Do you have cake? I woke up this morning craving cake. Lemon cake, with drizzled lemon icing and coffee. Ooh", she trilled as her attention shifted to the book in Varin's hand. "Is that *In The Middle Of The Night*? I brought *Attack of the Deranged Mutant Killer Monster* with me. I want that". She grabbed it quickly from Varin's hand. "Do they have any others? *Something under The Bed Is Drooling* or *Yukon Ho*?"

"You got me mixed up by calling it *Endless Nights*, Ma. Turns out that's the name of an Agatha Christie," Varin laughed. "And they have *Yukon* if you want another copy but Anjali said you have it at home. May I introduce my mother, Sanjana", he turned and said to Raqia's dad before he turned back to his mother. "Major Singh taught us at NDA. He went missing around Kargil. We were all very happy to hear that he had survived", he said diplomatically.

Raqia, like her brothers, could hear the unspoken questions that he didn't voice – like where had her father gone; and why had he disappeared for twenty-three years? How had he suddenly been found in a remote village in Punjab just this side of the border? The army had asked them all those questions when they'd gone to Raman uncle with the photo off Facebook that Mayank had spotted. It had taken the Major into custody for nine months after they brought him to Delhi, and they must have asked him all those questions, and he must have answered correctly because they released him with half the pension due to his rank. The three of them couldn't ask him any of those questions again because they were supposed to be so happy that their father was back.

"Pleased to meet you, Aunty. We do have lemon cake", Mayank said cheerfully. "Baked fresh this morning. You'll love it. I'm Mayank, by the way. And that's...", he turned to bring Raqia into the conversation.

"Your elder sister, Raqia", Varin Paranjape's deep voice cut off her brother's. His dark eyes met her startled ones. "All grown up. We last met in NDA. You were fourteen and the smartest person in the academy. We were all sure that you were going to become Dr. Raqia Bareja...or Dr something, very soon". Another warm wave rose through Raqia. But this one felt like she would float away on it. He put out his hand. Feeling like she was in a dream, Raqia put her hand into it. It was covered with calluses, but it felt right. Strong. Like she didn't want to let it go.

"She's still the smartest person in the room. She's a scientist with the Army's new tech team in Delhi. And she's here to give a series of lectures", Abhay laughed as he came up and shook Varin's mother's hand. "Hi, I'm Abhay and I'm studying law in Delhi." He turned back to Varin Paranjape as if magnetically drawn by his aura. "I remember you. We all looked up to you".

Varin Paranjape smiled at her brother but immediately turned back to her. He hadn't let go of her hand. "Lecturing", he asked with a raised eyebrow. "Where?"

"A couple of places including the Doon University. But officially, at IMA", her ever-cheerful younger brother piped in proudly.

"About what"?

'This isn't good. He's ex-army,' she frantically thought, 'I'd better keep quiet.'

"Didi, Maggi?" Kirpal was saying when she finally managed to focus on reality and the bowl he was holding out. It wasn't the first time he seemed to have said it because there was pin-drop silence as everyone stared at her expectantly. Luckily, the moment she took the bowl, Varin freed his hand and smoothly turned to Abhay without waiting for her answer.

'Oh, God. I hope it wasn't me holding on so tight that he couldn't get away. I hope I didn't creep him out, she thought with a mental cringe. 'Oh, Raqia. Way to go'.

Abhay carried on as if nothing had happened. "And I'm studying law in the morning and interning at a lawyer's chambers in the afternoon in Delhi. But dad decided to come down to Dehradun with Raqia for two weeks and I followed. Unfortunately, now that I'm here, all I want to do is sleep", he laughed.

"Oh, then it's not fair to ask you to drop me at the institute", Raqia exclaimed. "I'll drive myself. Will you all be okay without the car for a while? But I need to leave now. Where's my license? Oh gosh, I'm so late". She started spooning the hot Maggi into her mouth but could only eat a couple of forkfuls. In the meantime, the noodles hung down from her mouth and she had to inhale them sharply. She suddenly realized what she was doing as the lady in front of her grinned widely.

"Oh, Varin will drop you", Mrs. Paranjape said sweetly. "And you can eat your Maggi in the car".

"What are you doing there", Raqia asked in confusion.

"Just visiting ", her son said unhelpfully. "Yes, of course, I can drop her", he told his mother dutifully as he removed his fascinated glance from Raqia's full mouth and looked at his mother. "But what about your lunch...will you be okay?"

"I'd be absolutely ecstatic here with my new book, some pasta, and that lemon cake", his mother said with shining eyes. "I wanted to go up to Welham. I studied there for a few years", she confided to them. "But my parents decided to go abroad and pulled me out. I loved it there. My sister didn't. And I hadn't been one of those Vikrams in years. Doon's changed so much. I could barely recognize it", she'd already seated herself on a table and the Major had to perforce join her.

"No, no", Raqia said in horror to the waiting Varin. "I'll find my way. I have to get back as well".

"I'll pick you up", Mayank promised just as Varin Paranjape spoke. "I'll drop you back. We're staying at the Mess outside town so we had no plans today".

"Oh, then I can show Mrs. Paranjape around tomorrow morning. There's so much to see. And dad grew up here. He'll know the old places", Mayank said excitedly. "Sure", Abhay added enthusiastically to Raqia's dismay, "I've got to go back tomorrow night but Raqia's got work till Friday so she'll help"

"Oh? We're here till Friday", Varin Paranjape said with a raised eyebrow as he turned to stare at Raqia. "But what time is your class today? Should we get going?"

"Oh Jesus", Raqia gave a little shriek as she peeked a look at her watch. "But I can't put you out like that. You must stay with your mother. You can't spoil your plans for me".

Everyone just ignored her. Abhay was already packing her laptop and papers into her satchel while Mayank vanished and came down a minute later carrying her purse.

"I need to go to the loo, idiot", she half-whispered and half yelled as she ran upstairs past him. "We're going to talk later". He looked genuinely confused.

# CHAPTER TWO

A few minutes later, she found herself standing in front of a high Mahendra jeep. It fit Varin Paranjape's height.

He was carrying her bowl of noodles which he handed her as soon as she put her purse and laptop in the back seat and climbed in.

"Thank you, Major Paranjape", she said formally as he shut her door and went around.

"It's Colonel. But just call me Varin", he smiled at her before putting the car in motion. "We're old friends."

She looked at him in silence for a minute. 'Were they old friends? They'd never actually spoken, as far as she remembered. And why would he have noticed her? She'd been fourteen while he'd been at least twenty-five. It would have been a little creepy if he'd noticed her'.

"Twenty actually", he said softly, seeming to read her mind. "I was pretty young but Dad was posted abroad and I was at a loose end. And I looked older than I was. So, I joined up. And you were a pretty...pretty little thing".

She blushed.

"I thought you may have dropped out of the army", she confessed. "I followed your career for a couple of years but then lost track".

"The famous 'punched the CO' episode", he smiled. At least his mouth twisted into something that resembled a smile although he kept looking at the road. "No. Luckily, his boss also thought he was a jerk so I got let off with a warning. My son is twelve now. Lives with his mother. She's...well, she's gone on to bigger and better things".

"Oh, you're both not together", she asked seriously.

He turned to look at her. His aviators hid his eyes and mirrored back her face so there was no way of knowing what he was thinking.

"She cheated on me while I was away. In my marriage bed. I'd still have stayed but she wanted her freedom. I ran wild for a few years afterward, hence the tattoos, but I'm fairly sober now. I still love my son and daughter but I'm an army man. So of course I had to give her and her new husband custody".

Raqia blinked. It was hard to listen to the sudden bleakness in his voice.

"I'm fine now although it took a while", he continued. He looked back at the road. "But I went through all the phases. Drink, gambling, women. Lost all my money. It took my old CO and a couple of my NDA pals to take me in hand and pull me back. Although the kids are my life. And now Ma is back. She decided to live in Delhi so that she's close to me. Perhaps if I can prove that I can provide a stable household, I'll get custody back".

Raqia froze the moment she heard the words stable background. She could see her life ahead raising another generation alone in Dehradun if she took on Varin Paranjape's two children. All she wanted was to get away. She wanted to have fun. She wanted to be gambling in casinos and drinking in shady bars. Not raising more children while her husband vanished as her father had.

She hurriedly took a large bite of the congealed Maggi in her hand. It was cold but she still sucked all the strands in and started chewing on them. Varin stilled as his attention focused on her mouth again. Suddenly Raqia felt weighed down as if the car seemed filled with heavy air. There was a feeling like thunder and lightning was going to strike inside the car.

A car honked near her ear and they jumped. "Shit", Varin cursed as he swerved the steering wheel right and out of the way of the auto overtaking from the wrong side. The driver glared and the twenty-odd kids piled into the back of the overloaded auto waved cheekily as they went past. Raqia had to smile back.

"Kids from the hills are cute, aren't they", Varin Paranjape said huskily next to her. She looked back to see him looking intently at her and smiling slightly. She blushed. 'He's pretty cute when he smiles. He was always pretty cute when he smiled. And he used to smile a lot, she remembered. 'No, wait. Jis rah par chalna nahin, wahan jaana kyun'? She shook her head slightly and smiled back impersonally.

Varin Paranjape blinked and looked confused for a minute. He turned his head back to the road and took a deep breath. There was a silence in the car. Raqia took another determined bite of her Maggi and chewed on it stolidly.

"So, your dad", Varin tried again. "When did he get back? Did he say where he was for so long? Everyone's very curious. It's rare for someone to make their way back after twenty-something years. And even more rare to be fine."

Raqia stiffened. 'What do I say,' she wondered. 'Do I toe the official line or say what I'm feeling? I don't know him, not really. A little flirting is a dangerous thing but not as dangerous as what I'm thinking.

"He got back four months ago", she said woodenly. "Or rather, we got him back four months ago. The army kept him for a month in hospital and nine months for debriefing in Delhi or somewhere."

"You were too young", Varin murmured.

Raqia took a deep breath and words long held back just started spilling from her mouth. "I was fourteen and a half when he disappeared, and the boys were barely four. Our grandparents took us in. My grandmother died while I was at Oxford and I had to come back to take care of my grandfather and the boys. I was twenty-five then. I've been here ever since, living in Dehradun and then Delhi and working as a researcher and trainer with the Army. I'm grateful dad's friends got me in. It's a decent job. It helped me to raise the boys while looking after my grandfather and the bookshop, even though it wasn't easy. The opposite of your story, really". She looked out of the window. "About the Major, well, it's good to have an answer one way or the other. We were stuck in limbo, unsure if he had deserted or died. But his being back takes some getting used to. And at least, now we get half his pension", she leaned back in the seat and smiled grimly as she raised her arms in a shrug. She'd forgotten that she was still holding the bowl of Maggi. It tipped sideways and she had to scramble to righten it. A few strands of congealed noodles slid down. They both watched in horror as they slid down the clean leather seat, fell across the gearbox, and slipped under both their seats. Varin Paranjape whimpered for a couple of seconds before he slammed his mouth shut, but he couldn't hide the look of anguish on his face. "Oooooh God", Raqia wailed. "I'm so sorry. I'll pick it all up". She dived down to look under her seat, forgetting that she was wearing a seat belt. It was only when she couldn't bend that she remembered it. With a red face, she kept the hated bowl of Maggi on the dashboard, opened the belt, and bent over.

A few strands had got under both seats. Unfortunately, the ones on Varin Paranjape's side were between his feet. She went for those first so that he didn't step on them and grind them into the mats. But it was a big car. To do that she had to push herself past the gearbox.

"What are you doing", Varin yelped as he looked down. Raqia suddenly realized that her nose was touching his thigh as her hand groped the floor for Maggi. But she couldn't get up without picking up the slippery noodles which were moving backward as her fingers touched them. "Looking for noodles", she grunted, focused on the job at hand.

Varin relaxed. She could feel his thigh unclench itself. "I thought we were getting friendly real fast", he drawled, a smile in his voice. "Hmm", she replied, preoccupied with the noodles. "Almost got that one. Just one more", she said as she finally grabbed the second last strand. Of course, the last strand had slipped backward past Varin's boot. She made a determined effort to elongate herself and reach it. His thigh was too thick. Her nose, and therefore the rest of her couldn't reach the strand.

He bent down and picked up the noodle. He was holding it up as she rose, a grin on his face. "That was awfully friendly of you", he grinned as he carefully parked the car on the side of the road. "We're almost at the gate. I'd hate for the Jawans to see me drive in with a girl's head in my lap".

Raqia looked around blankly, and then with dawning horror. "Your hair", Varin pointed out. She looked at him and blinked, unable to understand what he was saying. He sighed. "Brush your hair. Fix your lipstick, and clothes now. We're almost at the gate. And if anyone asks how we know each other, tell them we know each other from NDA days".

"But that's how we know each other", she protested. "Wait, how are you going in? You're ex-army, aren't you? You said you're visiting Dehradun".

He ignored her questions as he leaned past her, opened the dashboard, and handed her the brush that he took out. He then pulled down the visor so that the mirror showed. "Clean up", he ordered. "We'll continue the conversation on the way back".

She meekly took the brush and stared at it. It was a woman's hairbrush. With a hair in it. She looked more closely. It was a white hair. "Oh, your mum's", she blurted in relief.

"You're amazingly smart about some things and dumb about others, aren't you", the big man sitting next to her laughed.

She bristled but before she could say anything, he pointed to his watch. "We're late. Hurry up please".

He stared at her as she looked in the mirror. She was horrified by what she saw. Her front hair was standing up as if she'd been through a hurricane. Once he was satisfied with the way she looked, he started the car and drove up to the gates.

The Jawans saluted. "Colonel Varin Paranjape from Delhi HQ and Dr. Raqia from Delhi TRC", he said calmly as he pulled out his badge from a cubbyhole in the dashboard and showed it to them. They opened the gates and stood to attention. Varin Paranjape saluted back. Raqia was in shock; unable to say anything.

He drove in silence till they reached Chetwode Hall and stopped in front of it. "Nine, eight, seven, two, four, four, one, eight, three", he rattled off. "I'll wait for you at sixteen thirty hundred hours here to take you home. Call me if there's any change in the program", he instructed as he stopped with the sound of gravel flying. Raqia found herself having to get out of the car in front of the cadets and officers who were walking into the building. Several of them saluted Varin Paranjape, she noticed. Most of them studied under her. 'They're all staring at me,' she wailed to herself. 'I can't believe I'm going to have to walk past their knowing smiles. Yuck."

She opened the back door and grabbed her laptop and purse from the seat. "Ummm, the Maggi", she asked. "Don't worry. I'll have the bowl washed out", he promptly replied. The moment she stepped back from the car and slammed the door, he drove off, leaving her feeling flustered and off-balance as she quickly walked into the building.

As she tip-tapped quickly down the hallway, she had to pass some of her students. They saluted and she had to nod as she quickly walked past. 'They're purposely walking slowly so that they can check out what's happening. What an idiot I am not to have got off outside the gate,' she thought sullenly as she made the long walk of shame past them down the long corridors.

The seated cadets greeted her with smiles when she entered the class. Her blood pressure slowly lowered as she set up her laptop with her face down. 'I'm not taking a lift home with him,' she vowed. 'Not in front of the class.' A vision of a closeup of his thick thigh danced in front of her eyes, making it very difficult to concentrate on her notes.

He suddenly appeared at the door, but this time in uniform. The entire class immediately stood up and saluted. "At ease. Sit down please", he said as he walked to the back of the class and took a chair. When the cadets sat down this time, their demeanor had changed. A senior officer was present.

To his credit, he was completely invested in the class, even asking pertinent and serious questions. The problem was that Raqia was so flustered that she had no idea what she was saying.

Colonel Aggarwal – a member of the Administrative staff she couldn't stand, suddenly appeared at the door. Without apologizing to her for disrupting the class, he looked at Varin Paranjape and jerked his head. The man blinked, inclined his head, and got up...and up. 'My God, he keeps getting bigger, Raqia thought in disbelief. 'He's as wide as he's tall. Even in a class full of officers. That's the problem. They are so much younger. And inexperienced'.

The entire class immediately stood up as he walked past them. "At ease. Carry on", he said quietly and they all sat. "My apologies for leaving midway", he apologized to her as he stood at attention in front of the class. "It's work. I'll try to attend the next class tomorrow. Thank you". He walked out quickly, leaving her feeling like a limp noodle. She had been painfully aware of him while he'd been there but now that he was gone, she already missed him and his questions. He'd probably asked more incisive questions in the...she quickly checked her watch, two hours he'd been in the class than she'd answered in the past...she checked herself. 'That's not fair," she lectured herself severely. 'The rest of them aren't dumb, and comparing Aggarwal to anyone will make anyone shine. Back to work, my girl. Do your job'.

She took a deep breath and looked around to realize she'd been silent for a while. The young cadets were openly grinning at her. She frowned and gave them a severe look. 'That man', she fumed. 'This is all his fault'.

She felt like she'd been put through a wringer by the time she walked out of the room an hour later and walked to the toilet. As she washed her hands, she found herself examining her face critically as she imagined someone else looking at her would. 'I look awful', she fretted. 'My hair is standing up all over my head like I've touched electricity'. Her mind sped back obsessively to his thigh and his brush. 'I know I have a brush in my Pandora's box,' she snorted to herself. Her brothers called her bag Pandora's box because it contained everything anyone could need. It had started when they were kids because she had to carry everything they may need and she'd never shed the habit.

While she was fishing around inside the bag for her brush, her hand hit a small tube. 'Lipstick', she decided. 'I haven't worn any in a while. It'll be a nice change. The cadets deserve to see me look good.'

It turned out to be tinted lip balm but no matter how much she dug into her bag, she couldn't find lipstick and she finally had to use the balm. By the time she opened her bun and remade it, she knew she was late but she didn't want to rush herself till she looked good.

She finally emerged to find a subedar waiting for her. "Salaam Saab", he saluted her. She saluted back with a sinking feeling in her stomach. Sure enough, he said the words she didn't want to hear. "Paranjape Saab is stuck with work. A driver is waiting outside to take you home. Your tiffin box is in the car". He saluted and turned sharply before walking away leaving her feeling upset, annoyed, and sad all at once. 'I should be used to waiting for army officers by now', she lectured herself. 'I've waited for dad to come home for so many years.

An army jeep was waiting for her at the steps. The driver saluted as she got into the back where her newly cleaned bowl and fork were lying in solitary splendor. They started the drive back in silence.

Her bag vibrated and she jumped before she realized that a message was coming in on her phone. She grabbed her bag and dug into the side pocket where she kept her phone. It buzzed again.

"Sorry, got called into work", said the first message. "Ma called to ask if you and the family would like to join us for an early dinner? We don't know anyone else in town and Ma is sick of Mess food", said the second. "Nineteen hundred hours", said the third autocratically. "Let me ask the family", she immediately wrote back without thinking, her good mood restored.

A minute later, she realized what she'd done. She had no idea what the man did except that he was senior enough to walk into a class and get saluted. Also, now that she thought about it, how had he got her number?

"Varin Saab is from which department", she casually asked the driver, not really expecting an answer. "Headquarters, ma'am", was the immediate reply. "NSG". She frowned. Her work did involve NSG but so far no one from there had attended any of her lectures.

"Oooooh. Varin", her very efficient and very gay brother replied when she called him. "He's so good-looking. Yea, I'm in. Hold on. Hold on. Dad's still with Mrs. Paranjape. They haven't got back yet. I was asking Joginder to fix dinner. Should I stop? Abhay's watching movies in his blanket at home. Can you call him"?

"I'll call him", Raqia promised as she put the phone down. 'Why didn't I think of the fact that Mayank would like the attention he was getting from a good-looking older man,' Raqia thought, shaken by the fact that her brother liked Varin Paranjape as well. 'Oh, well, when in doubt....',

"Abhay", she spoke quietly into the phone as soon as her brother answered. "Varin Paranjape wants to take us all out for dinner tonight. Seven. Why?"

"Well, perhaps because his mother spent the afternoon with me and the Major and it was good fun. They're still out. She's nice. I'm in", her brother said happily.

"Hmm...is the Major interested in her"?

"That would be nice, especially for you", Abhay said doubtfully. The Major tended to follow them, especially Raqia who was at home more than the boys, around like a lost puppy. He'd even offered to drop her at work and for her lectures. She hated it, and Abhay knew it. But there wasn't anything they could do. His only other interests were the laptop they'd got him and television.

She rang the Major next. He was on a busy street and she could barely hear him. "Ji, are you out somewhere", she inquired as soon as he answered. "Yes", he puffed. "Mrs. Paranjape wanted Kwality toffees so I offered to bring her here for tea". "Do call me Sanjana", she heard in the background. "Are you okay", she asked in concern. 'He certainly hasn't shown any inclination to take us out for tea or toffees since he's been with us,' she thought in half indignant amusement. 'The only thing he's shown any interest in has been watching television and my work. This may be too much for him. I don't want him to go back to hospital', she thought in dismay. 'This mother-son combination is taking over our lives in just a day and I'm being unusually emotional today', she thought in frustration.

"Yes", the Major laughed. 'He laughed', she thought in disbelief. 'He hasn't laughed in so many days.'

"Would you like to go for dinner with Sanjana and her son", she asked cautiously.

"Not today, baba", her father said promptly. "I will need to rest after this".

She called Abhay back. "Dads not coming but Mayank is", she reported, very aware that the driver was hearing every word and would give the details to whoever asked.

"Then I'd better come", her brother yawned. "Mayank in love is a fun sight to see. He hasn't stopped talking about Colonel Paranjape since you guys left. And I called some of the guys in Delhi. You do know he's high up in the NSG, right? Brass likes him in Delhi".

"Fine. Just get ready and I'll talk to you once I'm home", she said hurriedly.

By the time they cleared the traffic on Rajpur road, she was later than she'd expected and had to run straight up to get ready. Varin Paranjape, his mother and the Major were sitting in the drawing-room with glasses of whisky in front of them when she came down. Varin rose immediately and the Major also got up after a minute. He had changed back into the jeans that she'd been so close to sometime back, but now he wore a gorgeous black sweater on top that stretched at the right places and showed his pecs to perfection. He'd even washed his face and brushed his hair till they were both shining. They sat down as soon as she did.

Sanjana was the first to break the silence. "I hope the lecture went well? Varin said it was really informative. And thanks for keeping me company over dinner. Varin adores spices and I can never eat a whole dish so I have to eat things that burn my esophagus. Too many years of living abroad and eating bland food, I guess. At least with you and the boys there, we can share a few normal dishes". Varin's mouth turned up on one side as he took a sip of his drink but he didn't say anything. It made Raqia conscious. She purposely turned her body towards his mother.

"Did you have a nice time today? I heard you went to Kwality ", she asked politely.

"Yes, I really wanted the toffees. I missed the fudge and the stickiness so much, I used to make Varin bring them to me. Other people ask for Old Monk from India. I just wanted my stick jaws", Sanjana laughed. "And the tea was lovely too. It was nice to visit my old favorites."

"It was tiring but nice", the Major added quietly. "I haven't walked so much in a while. It was the company that made me feel I could do it".

Sanjana beamed back at the Major. "That's what friends do. They encourage each other. You came with me. I got you good food". She turned back to Raqia and Varin. "Incidentally, Varin's taking me up to visit Paonta Sahib tomorrow morning, if you'd like to come along?"

"I don't mind coming", Mayank said from behind her as he rushed out of his room. "We haven't been in ages." Raqia kept quiet, although, like Mayank, she would have genuinely loved going to the 19th-century gurudwara which was built next to the river. She hadn't been there for a long time.

Varin looked at her appraisingly before he turned to the Major. "Are you sure you wouldn't like to join us for dinner? We aren't going to be out late."

"I'm a bit tired", the Major admitted. "Perhaps some other time. All I want is some dal roti and my bed".

"I'm glad you enjoyed yourselves today, dad", Mayank said cheerfully as he came forward-nattily dressed in brown brogues, a blazer, and a black turtleneck, his mustache swinging upwards and his beard carefully coiffed. Abhay came down the stairs as well, still wrapped in his blanket but wearing bright red jeans and sneakers. The twins were a contrast in styles. Mayank looked at Abhay in confusion. “Are you going to go dressed like that? They won’t allow you into the restaurant”, he warned.

“Of course, not”, his brother said indignantly. “I plan to leave the blanket at home.” He shook his head sorrowfully. “Some people have no faith in their siblings. Brother, I’m an advocate and man about town. I have a reputation”. Mayank rolled his eyes as he went to look at his grandfather’s whiskeys. “Do we have time for a drink”, he asked.

“We have a reservation for nineteen thirty hours”, Varin said, standing up. “Mum needs dinner. She hasn’t eaten and she’s had a long day today. And I’ve chosen a place that’s I haven’t been to before because it seemed popular”.

# CHAPTER THREE

The goodbyes would have stretched out but Varin herded them all into the car and got them to the restaurant in super quick time. The restaurant served Italian food mainly, belying Sanjana's story about spicy food.

"So, tell me about your father", he asked as they nursed their drinks. "What happened".

The siblings looked at each other. Abhay was the one who spoke up. "He got lost just before Kargil. We don't know the details. All we knew was that he said that he'd been called by Delhi a few months before Kargil for reconnaissance since he spoke Urdu and Punjabi. He called us before he left, and that was the last we heard from him, till he called some months later from somewhere noisy saying that he was okay. It sounded like a market place and we could hear Punjabi being spoken in the background. And that was it. We didn't know what had happened to him for twenty years. Then two years ago, a friend of Mayank's posted a picture of his Nani's house in his ancestral village outside Abbottabad on Facebook. Mayank brought it to us saying an elderly male servant in the background looked familiar. Like our grandfather. We sent the picture to Raman Uncle".

"Brigadier Aulakh", Mayank interjected. "He's in Intelligence".

"After a few days", Abhay continued, "he called to say that they'd picked up dad based on the photo. Turned out he'd been hiding there and kept putting off getting to a town or the border because he'd been thrashed a couple of times so he'd kept running further inwards, and he'd seen other suspected spies lynched. Often perfectly innocent men. The only thing that had saved him was the friend's Nani who was a tough lady and told the villagers and Daroga that she'd seen him in a dream and that he was a Sufi. He was pretending to be a wandering mendicant by this time so it fit. Also, he was there before Kargil so he was familiar to the villagers by the time Kargil happened. But those wandering days meant no food or shelter for months. And the villagers had been close to taking him to jail and lynching him when the lady intervened. After that, he just did whatever small tasks the family asked him to so that he'd have food and protection. There must have been much more that happened to him because, when we met dad, he was very confused. And that was months after he'd been brought back".

"But you believe that's your father", Varin Paranjape asked quietly, sitting forward in his chair and staring straight at Abhay. Raqia glanced at his mother. She hadn't said a word but tears were streaming from her eyes. Raqia felt like crying as well. This was every army wife and mother's nightmare. "We got him back", Abhay said after a minute. "It's been a lifetime. He'd probably given up hope or genuinely forgotten us. Either way, he's nothing like what I remember, but I was four when he left".

"He's my father. He looks like my grandfather", Mayank said staunchly. "He's got some of the same mannerisms when he forgets to be scared. I'm the one who spent the maximum time with Bade Papaji and Dad looks like a younger version of him. I know he's Dad."

Abhay kept quiet.

Varin glanced at her. "And you", he asked. "What do you think"?

"I think I'm glad to get his pension again", Raqia said promptly. "As long as he was in no man's land, we didn't have closure or money. And these boys and the bookshop eat a lot".

There was a moment of unguarded laughter as Mayank and Sanjana laughed helplessly. Even Abhay smiled. Varin did not. He stared at her levelly till she finally looked down and hurriedly broke a piece of the garlic bread.

'I keep thinking of my son stuck in that situation", Sanjana said as she wiped her eyes with a napkin. "Every army mother's nightmare".

"So, what do you do", Mayank asked Varin curiously.

"I'm with the NSG in Delhi. Home Affairs", Varin replied, looking levelly at Mayank.

"What does that mean", Abhay challenged him. "Home Affairs", Varin smirked. "Kitchen and so on. No. It's protecting the security of the nation. Too many threats this side".

"So, your office is in HQ", Raqia asked. "I'm based out of the RK Puram office". "I know", Varin said offhandedly as he called the waiter and ordered coffee for them all. Abhay and she looked at each other, confused. 'He knows that I work for the army and where I work', Raqia thought in alarm. 'Why? He's senior enough to attend and understand my lectures. He's NSG. What's going on?'

"So, you are in Dehradun on work", Abhay asked.

"No", Varin replied just as Sanjana added. "I wanted to see the city. It's changed so much since I was there. I wanted to go to Welhams and take a Vikram again".

“So, where do you live in Delhi”, Mayank asked, completely unconscious of his sibling’s growing discomfort.

“I’m in the Mess. Ma’s taken a house in Hauz Khas”.

“Oh”, Mayank said happily. “That’s not far from us. We stay in Hauz Khas Village. It’s an apartment but very nice. Raqia’s friends’ mum did it up at the same time as she did the bookshop. And the Village has all these water bodies and old monuments that are fantastic to explore. Where in Hauz Khas are you, ma’am?”

“It’s an old place near Chausat Khamba”, Sanjana replied. “I’ve got potters as neighbors so it’ll turn into a little artist colony, I hope”.

“I’d love to visit”, Mayank gushed. “And maybe bring dad. Bade Papaji’s always used to tell us that dad loved books and art and he’s not been interested in any of that since he returned. Maybe you could spark his interest in those things again”.

“Oh, that would be lovely”, Sanjana said happily. “I’m just setting up and there’s so much to do. I would love company”

The waiter brought the coffee and Raqia started spooning sugar and milk into hers. Varin put his cup forward and she gave him a startled glance. “I take a heaped spoonful of sugar and plenty of milk please”, he said playfully. When Raqia filled the cup and handed it back, their hands touched under the plate and a spark went straight from her fingers down her spine. He seemed to take a long time to take the cup and saucer from her.

“So, are you like, Raqia’s boss”, Abhay asked, breaking the tension.

Their hands parted and Varin took a sip from the cup and saucer before placing it on the table. “That’s perfect”, he said warmly to Raqia. "You know how to make a Fauji's coffee". He turned to Abhay. "No. Not at all. We have different jobs. As far as I understand, Raqia is in procurement. But the lecture today was extremely interesting. I can see why her boss is so fond of her and recommended that she teach here".

"It's a lot of reading", Raqia said with a rueful smile. "That one lecture takes five hours of preparation. Luckily, the university here allows me to use their library. Between Claws, JSTOR, the Oxford library, this one, I get by".

"I like libraries", Varin mused quietly. His eyes met hers over the coffee cup that covered half his face.

"Speaking of...Did you hear about the cyber-attack on the NSG website today", Mayank asked excitedly.

Varin put his cup down abruptly. "Yes", he said quietly, but this time there was a tone of menace in his voice. "They think Pakistanis hacked into the system and wrote those messages. If they hacked into one of the most secure systems in the world, they wouldn't do it to write messages on the website. They would do it to get information and feed false information."

"I didn't know about it", Raqia exclaimed in shock. "When did this happen?"

"This morning", Abhay said briefly. "How did you miss the news? I'm surprised you didn't get emails from your boss?"

"So am I", Raqia exclaimed. "I was on the computer all day. But I didn't even hear about it at the institute".

"Well, that's odd", Mayank said. "It's out on social media".

"You didn't mention it earlier either", Raqia turned to Varin in confusion.

"Nothing to mention yet", he said briefly. "I'd rather catch the people doing it. If it's Pakistanis, well, then they would be up to more mischief. If it's kids, they'll be taught a lesson. And if it's an inside job", his voice lowered menacingly. "Then we'll see".

"There's a lot of people with access to the system now", Raqia agreed, a little taken aback by his vehemence.

"You're bringing work home again, Varin', Sanjana babbled. "It's funny. Despite his huge size, he'll never fight anyone physically if he can help it...well, apart from the one episode that we all know, and he was mad with fear at the time. But his mouth gets him into all sorts of trouble".

Varin sat back and took a deep breath before he took a sip of his coffee.

Raqia relaxed as well now that she wasn't being attacked. She felt an urge to stare at his mouth. It looked like it got him into all sorts of trouble, especially when he gave that half-smile that was playing on his lips now. Just not the trouble his mother was thinking of.

"Tee-hee", Mayank laughed nervously as he shifted uncomfortably. "I don't think that's a problem", he giggled. "When you're so handsome and strong, you get forgiven a lot". His eyes brightened as he stared at his new crush.

Varin's eyes widened for a minute and his eyes narrowed as he looked at Mayank.

Raqia and Abhay's eyes narrowed in tandem. Mayank was the baby of the family. They'd spent a lifetime protecting him and if anyone insulted him, that person immediately made two enemies for life.

"Am I handsome", Varin asked quietly. "I hope I'm more than that. I hope I raise kids who love me enough that if I have to go to war, they wait for me and look for me for twenty years. And open their homes and hearts as openly as you all have. He's very lucky to have you three, especially you, Mayank. I can imagine what a fight you had to convince people to go and pick up a man from well inside Pakistan based on a photograph and your gut".

Sanjana reached across the table and caught her son's hand. She was crying openly. "The kids love you. You know they do. They've told me often that they want to live with you".

"Yes, but I can't keep them, can I", Varin snapped before he took a deep breath. "It's a bit of a catch 22. I love my kids and I want them to love me but I get to see them twelve times in a year. Because I'm an army officer, I can't give them a stable home".

There was silence around the table for a minute that Mayank broke. "Your kids don't live with you", he asked.

"No. I was telling your sister the story today", Varin replied huskily but with his small trademark smile back on his face. "But I learned to cook so that they want to visit me more often".

"Oh, he's a fantastic cook", his mother enthused. "You should all try his cooking. Especially his mutton. You'll lick your fingers."

"One day, Inshallah", Mayank teased him and Varin smiled back slowly.

The bill arrived and Varin insisted on paying.

"Anyone for a paan? Can't come to Dehradun and not have a paan", he asked as they got into the car.

"Of course, we'll come with you. There's a nice on the way home", Abhay said politely.

"I'd love to try your cooking", Mayank said happily as they drove back after the paan and toffees that Sanjana had inside the car. "Jitender and Kirpal cook well, but homemade food, mmm. We love the food in our house.

When you come to the restaurant next, we'll treat you to some food that'll blow your brains. Especially the mutton chops and the sandwiches". He looked around the car. "You know what we should do? We should go to Landour one day and eat at Mudcup, Ivy, Bakehouse, and Emily's and compare food. Spend a day up there. Have you been, ma'am? We can do it from Delhi as well. It's not far."

"Hmm, what I want to do is spend a couple of days, or a week maybe in Rishikesh", Sanjana said wistfully. "Get up and do yoga in the morning, spend the day by the river painting, eat those samosas, lie in the grass in Maharishi's ashram, eat chaat and besan laddoos at Gita Bhawan and wake up to chants. Especially since it's Shivratri soon. My husband and I did it once when we were courting and I've never forgotten it. He asked me to marry him up there. On Shivratri". She looked at her son. "Let's go down there then. It's been so long".

"Shivratri is a couple of months away", he shrugged.

"There's a yoga festival there at that time every year, Ma'am", Abhay interjected. "And there are a lot of religious leaders who come as well. As well as singers etc. I believe last year there was an evening when Rekha Bharadwaj performed and even Katrina Kaif came. The governor is supposed to be there. It may be sensible to book now. It won't be easy to get a room at short notice".

"Oh", Sanjana turned around. "I just wanted quiet. Maybe I should go now. I can go alone for a week. I'm not too old".

"Why don't you ask dad", Mayank said cheerfully. "Sitting by the river sounds like something he'll enjoy. And you both get along. I'll join Varin when he comes down. I love Rishikesh. And Shivratri, with that statue, is just magical. Ooh, I'm already loving it."

"You didn't let me complete", Varin interjected. "I'll be happy to take you all to Rishikesh. But right now we're going to Poanta Sahib Gurudwara tomorrow morning and stopping at Khodri Dak Pathar for a picnic. It'll take us the morning, but Raqia's class is in the afternoon".

"Ooh", Sanjana and Mayank said just as Abhay said glumly, "I can't. I need to get back to Delhi". "I've got to study...", Raqia started when Sanjana jumped in.

"I'll ask the Major", Sanjana said eagerly. "He looks like he could use a friend. And I enjoyed his company today. He was so chivalrous. You know, making me walk away from the road on the way back". She shrugged and Raqia could see that Varin and she shared the same genes. "And I could use friends like you all. I'm so impressed by how you've all raised yourself and accepted him back into your lives after so long".

In the back seat, Raqia and Abhay glanced at each other but didn't say anything. When she looked up, she saw Varin watching them in the rearview mirror.

"And we can plan for Shivratri", Sanjana continued gaily, "It sounds fun".

"I'd love to", Mayank enthused. "I'll have to check if I'll get leave", Abhay mumbled. "And If it's on the weekend? If it is, I'll come". Raqia didn't say anything. Going on a holiday with Varin Paranjape was not going to happen.

Sanjana laughed "If it's meant to be, it'll be. Let's not worry about it too much. I'm sure my darling son will figure it out. Just tell the Major that we'll come to pick you all up by six-thirty tomorrow"

They turned into the driveway of their house and Mayank, Abhay and Raqia started to get out of the car.

"Raqia, hold on", Varin ordered as he got out of the car and stepped up to her. "Your brother has a crush on me. You better be there tomorrow morning and even in Rishikesh to make sure he doesn't try to get too close and get heartbroken. I like him and don't want that misread".

"Wha", Raqia blubbered, flustered. "When are we going to Rishikesh?"

"In a couple of months", Varin said impatiently. "Didn't you hear my mum? She wants to be there for Shivratri. I'm going to figure out rooms for all of us. Five rooms. I presume Abhay and Mayank can share a room? Or I'll get six rooms. Unless my kids want to come. They're in Bangalore. I'm not sure they'll get leave at this point but let's see. And my mother seems to like the Major. She's been very lonely since my father died and I'm glad she's found a pet project. We'll pick you up at six-thirty tomorrow morning and then I'll take you to the institute afterward. Did you say that you have to study tomorrow", Varin continued, changing topics till she was dizzy. "Let me know where. I'll take you there after the picnic. Goodnight. See you tomorrow".

For the second time that day, Raqia found herself standing outside the car utterly flustered as it drove away. Abhay and Mayank were standing on the porch with their arms crossed staring at her. For once they looked like the identical twins they were.

"What", she said defensively.

"Oh nothing", Abhay said drolly. "Just wondering what you both planned to eat for breakfast. You looked at each other like I look at my omelet".

"He's cute", Mayank said wistfully before he sighed and focused."Wanna grab some chai and meet on the roof", he suggested. This was a ritual that the three had developed. This was their time away from the world.

"Early start tomorrow", Abhay and Raqia said in almost the same breath.

Mayank sighed. "Fine. I'll wake you both up tomorrow morning. Maybe Guru Gobind Ji will help us all".

"Goodnight", Raqia said as she unlocked the door. She started going up the stairs before she paused, ran down, and grabbed both brothers in a hug. "We'll always have each other, regardless of who comes and goes".

"Goodnight di", her brothers chorused as they hugged her back in a three-way hug.

They looked up to see the Major standing on the stairs in his dressing gown and smiling shyly at them. "Did you all have a good dinner", he asked. "I'm sorry I couldn't come with you. That woman can talk. I couldn't...I got a little tired. But she just called again so I had to get up. Would you all want a drink or are you sleepy?"

The three of them looked at each other. "Of course, we'd love a drink", Abhay said diplomatically. "What would you like? A cup of tea or milk?"

"A whiskey, perhaps", the Major said. "It's been a long time since I had anything as good as that bottle we had earlier. What is it?"

"Uh, it's Amrut", Abhay said helplessly. "It's an Indian whiskey. Very warming. I think I have some brandy as well. Should I take that out? Do you want to sit here or on the roof? I can take out the angeethi."

"It'll be too much effort to take out the angeethi", the Major demurred.

"Nonsense", Mayank said vigorously. "Abhay will set it up. I'll make the whiskey. Di, what are you drinking?"

"The Baileys, obviously", Raqia said. "If I'm not going to sleep, then I might as well have the good stuff".

“Ooh, Baileys in front of the fire. I’m in”, Mayank said with relish. “Let me start setting up the terrace and take out the glasses”.

“What’s Baileys”, the Major asked curiously.

“A liquor. Whiskey based with cream”, Raqia said shortly, already planning her next day in her mind. ‘If she asked to be dropped off directly at the university and they ate a picnic along the way, she could cut short on her breakfast time and still be in time for classes. She needed to visit the library to prepare her lecture for tomorrow. It could be done. She knew what books she needed to refer to. But she’d have to go directly to IMA without stopping for lunch.

“Can I try it as well”, her father said softly.

“Of course,”, Abhay said from behind them. “Just head up and I’ll bring the drinks”.

“I...I’ll light the angeethi”, the Major offered. “Just tell me where everything is. I can do that”.

“I’ll call Jitender”, Raqia said with an internal sigh. ‘This is going to be a long night’.

“I enjoyed today but that Mrs. Paranjape was....very energetic”, the Major said shyly as they all finally gathered in front of the fire. “Then she called just now again to check if we’re going to Poanta Sahib tomorrow. She wants to go to Rishikesh sometime. She says she hasn’t been for a while. I’m not sure...”.

“Ooh, we were discussing that in the car just now”, Mayank said enthusiastically. “I’m in. Di, can we all go? It’s been a while.”

Raqia remembered Varin Paranjape warning her that she better be around to keep Mayank away from him and took a large gulp of her drink. “Yokai”, she mumbled.

“They’re very...friendly, aren’t they”, the Major said doubtfully, at the same time. “I’m surprised Colonel Paranjape even recognized me. What did they say over dinner?”

“They were complimenting us and then we were discussing the NSG website hacking”, Abhay said cheerfully. “Oh, I’d forgotten“, Raqia yelped. “What”, her father demanded fiercely - more fierce than he had ever been. “Nothing”, Raqia said, taken aback”. “I had to check something”.

“Dad, please don’t worry about being friends with Mrs. Paranjape”, Mayank said sweetly. “She’s sweet and looking for a friend and so arc you. That’s all that’s important. Not your sexes”, he finished wistfully. “There’s a lot that people can take in the wrong sense”. For once Mayank wasn’t as cheerful as he usually showed himself to be. Raqia’s heart went out to him. He’d endured a lot through his school days but remained himself – innocent and helpful. There were times when she felt he was stronger than her because he had never allowed circumstances to change him and make him cynical. “You’ve already lost twenty years. Are you going to spend the next twenty worrying about people? Because I don’t see people making an effort to spend time with you as Mrs. Paranjape has. And if you want to go to Rishikesh, let’s go. It’s just a yoga retreat and”, he finished sweetly, “we’ll be there in a flash to look after you if she comes on too strong”.

“Who is the father here”, Abhay said genially. “The youngest giving advice. Right, I’ve changed my mind. I’m heading back early. I can be in the first class by ten. You kids have a fun day tomorrow. And Mayank, say the word and I’ll get some kids to cover for you for a day. The youngsters in college are always looking for an outing.

There's one in particular who would be happy to help out. She's pretty and wouldn't mind a drive down", he winked.

"That's mean", Raqia exclaimed. "Asking one of your girlfriends to step in instead of taking her on a date".

"Oh, she won't mind", Abhay stretched himself as he strutted. "Girls like looking after me".

Raqia and Mayank rolled their eyes in tandem.

"I'm going to bed", she announced, gulping the dregs of her drink. "If we're all starting early tomorrow, we should all turn in".

"So, the Paranjape's seemed okay to you? They weren't asking too many questions about me", the Major anxiously confirmed.

"No Ji. Mrs. Paranjape and Varin seemed okay", she repeated dutifully.

"Hmm, Varin", Abhay mused teasingly. "Not Major Paranjape. Oookay".

Raqia hit him on the shoulder. "We just went out to dinner with him, you dolt. I can't call him Paranjape while talking to him".

"Why not", Abhay argued. "You call all the younger officers by their surnames".

"I teach them", Raqia said testily. Suddenly, the questioning wasn't funny. "In any case, I'll ask him tomorrow. Now goodnight".

She left a surprised family behind as she went down the stairs to her room. 'But I can't deal with so many questions and people and things, she whined to herself. 'I don't have any answers. I met the guy today. TODAY. And there's too much that's happened. He and his mother have pushed their way in so hard'. She giggled as she brushed her teeth and thought about her words. 'Well done, Raqia', she thought as she finally curled up in bed. 'Now you'll have images playing in your mind all night long.'.

She got into bed and opened her laptop to check on her messages. She had a message about the attack in her emails but strangely, she seemed to have read the message already. It showed light grey. 'I must have pressed something during the class', she grumbled to herself. 'A scientist and I can't figure out computers.' The same thing seemed to have happened in the past, she noticed. But it was only a couple of marketing emails that she may have inadvertently pressed on while going through her mails. Nothing of importance. Making a note to speak with her boss in the morning, she closed the computer and fell asleep.

# CHAPTER FOUR

She woke up because someone was sitting on her bed and shaking her. "Go away, Varin....", she mumbled. "Umm, Di", Mayank's voice spoke. She quickly took her face out from the blankets to see her brother's red face and the cup of tea he was holding. 'Is my face equally red', she wondered as she hurriedly sat up, tucked the blanket around her, and took the cup.

"I thought we could say bye to Abhay", Mayank said quietly. "So, I came to wake you up". "Of course, we should", she said heartily, taking a sip from her tea to hide her face.

"Do you like him", Mayank asked. She looked at him carefully. "Do you", she asked back. "Yes, but I don't think he's my type", her brother said carefully. "He was being nice, maybe because he was trying to get to you".

"I doubt it. He wasn't....", she paused. 'He had been pretty nice to her yesterday,' she realized. The darkness of night suddenly gave way to the earliest signs of dawn as her mood brightened. She must have smiled happily because Mayank looked taken aback. Just as suddenly she remembered the conversation over dinner and her world darkened again. "No, I don't think he was being nice to either of us because of me, but he could have been nice because he wanted information on the Major. Let's wait and watch what he does next", she said. Her voice must have been particularly sulky because Mayank grinned. "It's okay di. He'll come around and figure out its dad. I mean, that dad's dad. Oh, you know what I mean. Can we go?"

Raqia laughed at him as he stuck out his tongue at her and left her to change. She was down in fifteen minutes but by that time Abhay and the Major were already ready and waiting. The Major was in warm trousers, a blazer, and a cravat. He was better dressed than he'd been since he'd got home. He had a sheepish smile on his face.

"Wow", she said. "I was just admiring him as well", Abhay laughed.

Mayank walked out at that moment and Abhay and Raqia's jaws fell. Apart from the color of his coat and cravat, he and the Major were dressed exactly alike, down to the expensive brogues. He and the Major looked at each other and grinned. "You got into Bade papaji's clothes", Mayank laughed. "I recognize that coat".

"I don't fit into my clothes any longer", the Major said sheepishly. "I went through the trunks yesterday and found Papaji's clothes. If I am stepping out...They smell a bit of mothball but I got Jitender to air them last night over the coals. Do I look okay?"

"Hmm. Is it for someone in particular? Because if she doesn't notice how good you look", Mayank teased, "then other women in Delhi are going to notice you now". He laughed as his father blushed. "Perhaps we should go to polo matches in Delhi", Abhay added jocularly. "Lots of women to notice you there. They'll be on in Delhi now. Would you like to go? I've got a classmate whose brother is in the President's Bodyguards. I'll ask him for passes".

"No no", his father protested shyly.

'Hey Ram', Raqia thought, still flabbergasted. 'We have to take him shopping soon. We never needed to. He wasn't going out. We didn't know who he was. He had no friends. He never spoke to anyone. Maybe he never spoke to anyone because he had...'. She glanced up and met Abhay's eyes. He looked as sad as she felt.

"Okay Ji, I'm going to take my leave. See you all on Saturday", Abhay said cheerfully. "I'll see you out", Raqia said quickly.

They walked out to the car; Abhay and Raqia were both too flabbergasted to say anything. "I wasn't ready for that. He looks like Papaji, doesn't he", Abhay asked in bewilderment.

"Yes", she said before a wave of emotion she was keeping back slammed through her. "None of us knew him back then. He was just dad. He went to work and came back to us, took care of us, and put us to bed. We didn't know his tastes or likes or dislikes even though we lived with him. You boys were too young but I was old enough. Why didn't I know him? How do I know who he is now if I didn't know who he was then", Raqia asked in anguish?

"It's okay Di. We'll spend more time with him. We'll look after him", Abhay said as he kissed her forehead and got into the car. "Have a good time today. Don't worry too much about anything".

"Oh", Raqia jumped forward to stop him from driving off. "Emails came through yesterday. I didn't see them. My bad".

"Okay, bye", Abhay said as he drove off. A big jeep came down the road and stopped to let his car drive past. Varin and Sanjana Paranjape waved at Abhay as he drove away.

"Good morning", Varin Paranjape called out to Raqia as he stepped out of the car. He was wearing a sleeveless blue jacket over a T-shirt and baggy jeans. With his slightly wet hair falling over his forehead, he looked adorable. "Good morning", she called back. "Would you like to come in for tea"?

"No, I think we should hit the road", Varin said. "It's going to be a long day for you".

Raqia ran in and grabbed her laptop and purse. Mayank and the Major were already in the car while Varin waited outside for her.

"Ah", he said as he got in. "You said you needed to work after the trip"?

"Yes. If you could drop me at the university, I'll work in the library and go to the Academy from there", she said politely. "No problem. I wanted to spend time looking up some information as well", Varin said. "I'll drop everyone and come back. That way we can go to the Academy afterward".

"I don't want to join you both", Mayank laughed. "I have enough books to read already".

"Hahaha", Varin laughed good-naturedly. "Do you know computers well, Major? Or is it all difficult for you"?

"I know....not very much about computers", the Major said. Raqia and Mayank frowned. "You work on your laptop quite a bit", Mayank pointed out. "I've even seen you on Raqia's laptop". "I watch movies and read the news", the Major answered testily. "Who would I receive emails from? One day, when I get a job, I may need to learn computers properly but I don't know much right now".

"Oh, emails remind me", Raqia interrupted. "DD, my boss, had messaged me yesterday. Seems there was a departmental advisory about the hack. I must have read it but I don't remember opening it. Too much excitement yesterday".

"Hmm", Varin said. "Well, there's nothing you could have done about the hacking anyhow. I just wonder what else they did while hacking".

"It was probably kids, as you suggested yesterday", Mayank replied. "Right now, tempers are running high and kids are upset. Oooooh, look. Makhana. Have you both ever tasted it? Colonel, please stop", Mayank squealed. "You haven't lived till you've tasted it".

Varin looked for a place to get off the road while Mayank opened the window and waved down the man rolling a cart with the steel containers of the yellow soufflé. As soon as the car stopped, Mayank ran out and returned with leaf dishes full of the sweet and cold soufflé like substance. After that, the trip was all about loud discussions about food and memories.

Raqia got down at the library on the way back and gave Varin directions on where to find her. He was back within an hour. She could hear his deep voice ask for directions and then the heels of his shoes ringing on the wooden floor as he walked closer to her. She looked up and felt a frisson roll down her spine and the heat rising inside her as he got nearer. He'd taken off the jacket and his Henley was tight around his chest and she could make out his flat stomach under that. With all the walking around all morning, there were small patches of sweat on the front and the shirt had been pulled free from the jeans so that it hung outside.

"Nice place", he smiled as he came up to the table. She could smell him now – a mixture of his natural smell and the deodorant he'd used. "It reminds me of all the times I hung out in libraries waiting for my girlfriend while she was in college. We even had a favorite spot. Does this library have a make-out area?

"I...I don't think so", she stammered, shocked. "But I didn't study here. I studied in Delhi and came upon the weekends. I have no idea where kids would...hang out."

"Oh. I've always thought a library would be the perfect place to steal a kiss. Perhaps you could show me around", he suggested. "We can look for books on politics and urban warfare and we can see if there's any place that kids hang out".

She got up obediently and took a look around. Students and teachers alike were looking at them. "Okay, but could we walk a bit faster", she said hurriedly. "I don't want anyone asking questions about you. I haven't asked permission to be here in a while. I just walk in".

Varin preened and shrugged. "I'm not in uniform", he pointed out. "I'm being discreet".

She just looked at him and rolled her eyes before walking quickly inwards. He knew exactly what he looked like. The other women were salivating.

"What else are you interested in", he asked as he walked a few steps behind her. She turned around, ready to snap at him for being a creep and he held his hands up innocently, grinning all the time. "I just meant that you used to enjoy horse riding and martial arts in NDA. And I was impressed with your stamina this morning. So, I wondered if you still exercise".

"Yes", she snapped before she replied a bit forlornly. "I used to play polo in Oxford. One of the few women. But I've given it up. No time to practice. I still work out a bit."

"If you don't have anyone to spot you, happy to", he said gently. "I'm not too good at horse riding but I enjoy martial arts and working out. Happy to join you at the gym. Do you lift weights or only aerobics?"

She looked at him doubtfully. "Abhay spots me", she said firmly.

"Then I can offer myself for karate practice. Or cycling around Delhi. I'm pretty much on my own and would love intelligent company. Are we heading to that side?" He pointed to the section just beyond them.

"Yes. I'm impressed with your eyesight. But be prepared for a lot of dust. I'm the only one who goes to that section".

"Then let's go look at them", he suggested. "Just so that you can say that at least one more person is interested in them".

"Hahaha. Good idea", she said happy to be away from the peering eyes around them.

It turned out not to be a good idea. They had to be quiet since they were in a library. This meant that they had to stand close to each other and speak softly. They reached for books and turned out to have similar interests and views. Their hands touched as they showed passages to each other and argued playfully about opinions on authors and politics. When she was winning a particularly vociferous, but quiet argument, he tickled her playfully. She leaned forward to speak authoritatively into his face, so close that her lips touched his. There was a spark and as she backed away, there was a pause and then his lips followed hers. He drew back, offering her a chance to step away. She couldn't. Especially when he put his hand around the back of her neck and pulled her in for a kiss. Or when she attacked him and his neck after that. It took the determined coughing of the head librarian to break them apart. And a lot of apologizing.

"What...", she asked as they hurried out of the library towards the car park. She couldn't frame the rest of the statement. She was lost for words.

"Yes", he replied briefly.

"We're adults", she argued, mostly with herself; still seething with anger at the way the head librarian had spoken to them.

"Yes", he replied as he opened her door and stood there as she swung herself up. When she couldn't, he boosted her by putting a hand under her bottom and hoisting her. She frowned down at him at the unfamiliar touch but didn't say anything. She had too much on her mind.

"That was a really bad idea", she said as soon as he got into the car.

"I'm pretty surprised myself", Varin said briefly. "Maybe don't kiss me in a public place again".

"Me", she sputtered. And then went quiet. 'To be fair, you kissed him and when he offered you a chance to get away, you kissed him again. Be fair'. 'Well done you. That was....awesome", her second thoughts said. 'We're going off duty and thinking about that all day. Bye now.'

She had to grin. He stared at her as if she'd grown a second head. "Fair enough", she said.

He blinked. "What", he asked. "You agree you attacked me"

"My bad", she said, feeling like she'd drunk champagne and the bubbles were fizzing inside her.

She'd done something finally. It had been too long since she had worked between home and office. "I promise I won't do it again. Especially since you're a senior officer".

"Technically, you're not an army officer and we don't work in the same department", Varin Paranjape spoke softly. "But let's not do that. There are reasons. In any case, what were you saying about mails being read this morning", he asked as he started the car?

She frowned, "Oh, I probably made a mistake. I must have touched something and marked the mails as read".

"You've done that before", he enquired.

"A couple of times", she admitted.

"Recently?"

"Yes".

"How long have you worked with the army"?

"I was with Claws earlier. Then joined TRC about a year and a half ago".

"About the time your father was suddenly found", he inquired softly.

She looked at him in alarm. "What"?

"Never mind", he said immediately.

"The army vetted him after he returned, Varin. They vetted him for nine months", she protested.

Raqia felt a shudder roll down her spine and a moment of disgust before she controlled herself. "My patriotism and brains aren't in doubt", she continued sharply.

"Not at all", Varin Paranjape said diplomatically. "Now, have you eaten anything or should we stop for lunch?"

She stared at him and he looked back blankly, his eyes hidden behind the sunglasses that were back on his eyes.

"Chole bhature", he asked as they passed a Dhaba. "If you're okay eating from the side of the road? "

She took a deep breath. 'I haven't done anything wrong,' she reminded herself. 'My father may have been called a traitor all my life but they can't doubt me. I've tried to do the right thing all my life. I brought up the boys. Took care of the house. Came back from Oxford. I'm worthy'. All the fizz had died out. "Sure", she said softly.

They ate quietly, both lost in their thoughts. The only interaction was when he held the water bottle for her to wash her hands with.

By the time they got back into the car, Varin's mood had changed again. At the next red light, he spread his arm across the back of the seat and started playing with her earring. "So", he said lazily. "How long is your hair? You always have it in that prissy bun so I can never tell.

Reminds me of a librarian. You just need the spectacles." His fingers moved past the earring and started playing with her earlobe. Her earlobe must have had nerve endings that she didn't know about and they must have been directly connected to her stomach because her insides flipped over and butterflies started playing in her stomach. All her attention was on her ears. She'd never before realized that ears were erogenous zones.

The light finally changed and the car behind them honked. Varin reluctantly moved his hand back to the gears and moved the car. Raqia maintained her silence. She couldn't move from accusations of being a traitor to feeling sexy. They maintained their silence. Once he tried to hold her hand. She moved hers away resolutely keeping a picture of Oxford's spires in her mind. He quietly brought his attention back to the road.

This time he sat through her class and He dropped her home after the class. Where they found Sanjana, the Major, and Mayank rolling with laughter.

"You're finally back", Mayank cried when he saw them. "Jitender, bring tea and something to eat".

"Varin, we've decided to spend the day in Rishikesh on Saturday. That's okay, right? We can go back to Delhi on Sunday", Sanjana asked brightly.

"Ooh, wait till you hear what we've planned", Mayank said happily.

Over tea, he and Sanjana told them all about the day she wanted and even Raqia was impressed with the moment-to-moment planning the woman had done.

She must have looked worried that evening because her father knocked on her door at night. "I picked up a copy of '*Where The Wild Things Are*' from the bookshop", he said. "In case you want to read it together. Remember how we used to read it together when you were a kid".

"I want to hear it too", Mayank pouted from behind him. "I never got alone time with you as a kid. Abhay was always there".

"Okay", their father said equably. Raqia frowned. Mayank must have seen because he shrugged and moved down the stairs. "No, that's okay. Tonight can be for Raqia. She's always rushing around and you both haven't had a chance to sit down with each other in the longest time", he said as he disappeared back down the stairs.

"Would you like me to read it to you", the Major asked her. She sighed and nodded. This was proof that he was her father, wasn't it? No one else would know that he used to read it to her. This was the final proof that he wasn't a charlatan.

Her father pulled up a chair and pulled a blanket he'd carried over himself. He opened the first page. "That night Max wore his wolf suit and made mischief of one kind", her father read out before turning the page. "And another. His mother called him "wild thing". "I'll eat you up" so he was sent to bed without eating anything. That very night in Max's room a forest grew".

Her father read the book till the end before he got up. "See, it'll all be fine. I just needed some time and laughter to heal. Tomorrow when we meet Varin Paranjape, you can tell him you know me well", he stated. "Goodnight now".

"Why did you disappear on us", Raqia asked him tremulously as he headed for the door. "RAW", her father said from the door. He didn't turn around to face her. "They sent me and then left me there, the bastards. They wiped their hands off me. Goodnight".

Raqia sighed as she got up to wash her face. As she looked at her swollen eyes in the mirror, she made a decision.

Going back to her room, she called Abhay. “He’s dad. He knew he’d read to me as a kid. He says he was RAW but abandoned”.

Abhay sighed. “Hold on. I’m going to conference call in Mayank”.

A moment later, Mayank joined the call and Raqia repeated what she’d said. “You don’t sound happy, Di”, Mayank said.

“He also told me to tell Varin Paranjape that he’s dad. I mean it’s wonderful that he’s giving us proof finally. But why now?”

“Maybe being around Sanjana has cured his depression“, Mayank questioned. “Perhaps he’s finally coming around to being himself”?

“Varin Paranjape was asking me questions about how long I’ve been with TRC. And when the Major got back”, Raqia said grimly.

“He did that”, Mayank and Abhay sounded equally shocked. “And then”?

“That was it”, Raqia had to admit. “The moment I said that I wasn’t involved in the hacking, he stopped questioning me”. She thought for a minute. “But I think I’m going to set up a system to forward my emails to another account. I’m not comfortable with not receiving DD’s emails immediately.”

“Okay, then he trusts you. So, we’re going to Landour tomorrow morning for breakfast. And we’re on for Saturday morning for Rishikesh.”

“You’re all having fun without me”, Abhay groused. I’ll come up tomorrow evening so that I can come to Rishikesh the day after”.

“Sounds good”, Mayank yawned. “I’m sleepy. Goodnight then. See you early tomorrow, Di”.

Raqia put down the phone and made the necessary changes to her email box so that her mails were forwarded to another account. It wasn’t going to solve anything but it made her feel more in charge.

Mayank woke her up early the next morning and both he and Raqia were ready well in advance and waiting outside by the time Varin and Sanjana arrived. “ I adore Landour”, he explained as Varin gave him an amused look. “I write regularly to Ruskin Bond. His books framed my life as a kid growing up in the hills. So, Landour is the city of my childhood imagination. And the food is..”, he kissed his fingers in appreciation. His enthusiasm was so infectious and his knowledge about Landour so extensive that they all couldn’t help but have a wonderful time. Since it was the last day of the course, Raqia was more relaxed as well. There were just the usual readings and research she had to do before class and it didn’t take her much time. Varin was a delight in class – asking questions that related to her specific fields of interest, and her obvious knowledge in those areas shone through so that the cadets gave her a standing ovation when the class ended. Varin didn’t drive her home from the institute though, and he and his mother didn’t join them for dinner either. But Abhay did drive up from Delhi that evening and everyone was so excited about going to Rishikesh the next day, that Raqia didn’t have a chance to feel miserable.

# CHAPTER FIVE

It turned out to be lovely if a cold day in Rishikesh. Mrs. Paranjape had three yoga course venues she wanted to look at. Even as the Major demurred about joining a full month's course, she signed them both up at one that was near the Ram Jhoola bridge; and booked them into a hotel that overlooked the Shiv statue. She didn't like the first few places they went for lunch and she roped Varin and Abhay into asking the locals about the best non-oily food they ate. She had finished her whole checklist by lunchtime including a visit to the Beatles ashram. The only thing left on the list was a visit to Neelkanth temple, but there had been an avalanche and the locals refused to allow them to go. They would all have been happy to hang out on the small stretch of beach near the Jhoola but she insisted that they head for Valmiki's ashram.

It was a steep car ride but when they reached there, Raqia had to draw in a breath of wonder. The view of the mountains and the river was incredible. It was also a fairly steep climb down from the ashram on slippery rocks. The younger men still insisted on going in for a dip, and Sanjana and she decided to dip their ankles.

Varin, as he rose from the water was a sight that made her want to stop breathing and made her thirsty at the same time. The shirt he was wearing was soaked and his muscles were outlined by the wet cotton. His trousers clung to his thighs, but the long T-shirt covered everything crucial. Raqia had to pinch herself. 'Get a grip, girl,' she lectured herself. 'There was no way your brothers will let you live it down if they catch you staring'.

"That's not fair", he quietly stopped her as they both stepped out of the changing rooms together. "I showed you mine but I didn't get to see yours". He winked and was gone before she could gather her wits and say anything.

They found themselves rearranged on the way home. Mayank and she were in the car with Sanjana and the Major while Varin and Abhay bonded in his car.

"Right", Sanjana said as she turned to the Major on the way home. "Now I can go back to Delhi happy. I believe the kids are coming in tomorrow as well so I'll have a full house".

"You know, we were discussing Delhi", the Major ventured quickly. "And you mentioned that you're looking for advice on your garden in Delhi and...I thought, perhaps we could all help you set up your artist studio and garden. I mean, because you've just moved to India and are uncertain....", he trailed off.

Raqia felt her heart falter. Paranjape was not going to like this. She glanced at Mayank. Of course, he was grinning.

"Oh, this is such a lovely idea. I feel like we're already such good friends. And you can meet the children. Once they leave, the house will feel so empty", Sanjana confided. "Especially after being with you this week".

"Are you tired or do you want to go for dinner now", the Major asked enthusiastically.

Raqia had had enough.

"Or perhaps we should wait till we get to Delhi", she said slowly. "It's pretty cold and we have to travel early tomorrow".

"We can sleep in the car", Mayank argued and then shut up as his sibling turned her head to stare at him coldly.

"Yes", he meekly agreed. "Let's wait for Delhi".

The Major bowed his head and didn't say anything. Raqia knew she'd made the decision for everyone but it didn't stop her from being mad at the world.

She caught Varin alone when they were saying their goodbyes. "Could we speak whenever you're free? I need to say something".

"Sure", Varin said, surprised. "I'll call you as soon as I'm back at the Mess".

*****

"He's my father, Varin. He knows what books he read to me as a child".

"So, you don't believe he's a spy planted by Pakistan? And possibly using you as an entry point into TRC to find out and send back details", he inquired softly. "Because the hacking wasn't just about the messages left on the website. We're finding more anomalies. Information being sent on etc. And the timing was perfect".

"But I'm not privy to any top-secret information anyhow", she protested, feeling like she was in a bad dream.

"Yes, that's true. But you give him access to the system. And if he knows enough about computers nowadays, he can hold the whole system to ransom. In any case, we're looking at various entry points. Everyone is a suspect right now. He was just in the right place at the right time. But I'm happy that you've got proof that he's your father".

There was silence for a few minutes. Neither seemed to feel the need to fill it. Finally, Varin spoke. "You know I'm not very far away. Just a couple of kilometers as the crow flies", Varin's rough voice sent a frisson down her spine.

"Everyone's asleep. I'll pick you up. Come to me".

"You'll have to drop me back before four", she argued, giving in immediately. "Before the Jawans wake up".

"Can't you pretend you've gone to the Gurudwara early", he teased huskily before his voice roughened? "I'll drop you back. Before anyone wakes up".

*****

The night was incredible. They barely got any sleep before they had to find their clothes and quietly start the car. This time, when he reached for her hand, she allowed him to hold it for a little while before she reclaimed it. She needed that hand. To fill applications for her Ph.D. She was sick of taking care of people. Of being used. Buffeted by people including her father and Varin. He looked at her in silence but didn't say anything.

"The kids are coming into Delhi tomorrow. Come to the airport to pick them up with me", he said gruffly as she got out of the car.

"No", she said immediately. "Take Sanjana",

She could hear him sigh in the darkness. "Fine. I'll go on my own. But there's an exhibition at the museum. Come with me to that before I go pick up the kids. I can meet you there around thirteen hundred hours."

"What exhibition", she asked suspiciously.

"Buddhist art. International. Not at the museum as such. It's next to the museum. We can go in and see the miniature paintings after that. I love those".

"Okay", she said impulsively, not wanting to let him go. "I'll meet you there".

She crept into the house and up the stairs happy. It was already four and they would need to leave by seven-thirty. She resigned herself to managing with two hours of sleep.

*****

Even though Abhay had been staying in the apartment in Delhi, it was necessary to start washing clothes, cooking for the week, and opening mail. She still managed to make it to the museum by one clock. The exhibition turned out to be her next downfall.

# CHAPTER SIX

"I can't believe a Colonel in the army would behave like that", the Director of the Museum said severely. "If it had been anyone else, I would have thrown you both in jail. Children come through here. There were pictures of Gods on the walls. You both should have shown some respect; some decency; some common shame". He was practically spitting as he got more and more worked up. The rest of the staff in the room was smirking. Raqia hung her head as she pulled repeatedly at her handbag strap. 'What on earth did I just do', she thought as she remembered...everything. How good he'd looked as he'd waited for her to get out of her taxi. His hand touched hers repeatedly as they waited for the tickets and wandered through the statues and then the museum shop. He seemed to know a lot about art because he'd read catalogs over her shoulder and pointed out paintings he found especially interesting. One of the catalogs had been on Shiv and Parvati and the eroticism of the paintings had made her even more aware of him standing next to her and looking at the same works. When they'd started walking through the statues, there were some...too many, that was erotic in so many ways. Women sitting on men; couples kissing; Shiv holding Parvati's breast. It was life-size erotica in front of them.

She had no idea what happened in the miniature painting section. All she remembered was standing in a lonely quiet section looking at Kishangarh paintings with him breathing behind her. They must have touched. She must have turned. The next minute they were kissing while their hands moved all over the other person. Her living breathing statue had come to life. As gorgeous as a Gandhara God. 'I'm going to think of him every time I look at a statue from now on,' she lamented to herself. 'What is wrong with me?'

"You should think of your children", the Director was still droning on as she returned to the present. "What would they have thought?"

"Children", Varin blinked. "I have to pick up the children. They're arriving at the airport at sixteen hundred hours". "From where", the Director demanded. "Umm, from my wife's", Varin blurted.

The Directors' worst fears were confirmed. He looked at them both in disgust "Leave please and don't come back", he ordered.

They walked out in silence as the staff giggled and whispered and gave them knowing looks.

"I'm sorry about that", Varin Paranjape said quietly as they walked out. "I have no idea what came over me... again".

"I have no idea what came over me either", she said honestly. "But let's not talk about it ever again. And you need to get your kids now".

"Why don't you come with me? We...left the museum earlier than planned so you have time. And I can drop you home on the way back. And you're supposed to be coming for dinner. Your dad and Mayank are going to be there. And you promised to save me from him, remember. So that his heart doesn't get broken", Varin laughed.

Raqia looked at him sharply. "This is not something we're going to repeat. It was an aberration in Dehradun".

"Of course,", Varin said innocently as he herded her towards his car. He looked back at the museum exaggeratedly. "Of course, you need to stop attacking me. In any case, I don't expect you'll attack me again". He opened the passengers' door, waited for her to get in, and only then walked around to the driver's seat.

They were both silent as they drove. Raqia was uncomfortable but Varin was looking straight ahead. The road had no traffic lights so they kept driving in silence down Akbar Road till they finally had to pause as they hit the Ridge Road. It was a long pause including police and ambulance deployment.

"So", Varin said lazily as he spread his arm along the back of her seat and started playing with her earring. "What's your most ticklish parts? And the most erotic ones? I notice you kind of have trouble breathing when I do this". His fingers moved past the earring and started playing with her earlobe again. This time her body knew his fingers well and lit up on its own. Her insides flipped over and butterflies started playing in her stomach. All her attention was on her ears. She was starting to think that ears were undiscovered erogenous zones. His hand slipped lower and started massaging her neck. She melted. "Hmm, there's a lot of tension here. I'll have to do something about it", he said. The policeman gave them the signal to move. Raqia firmly reached out and removed his hand from her shoulder.

They kept quiet the rest of the way to the airport.

Thanks to his army identity card, they were allowed to go into the airport to receive the children.

"There they are", he said, as passengers started streaming into the airport from the flight. The boy turned out to be a gangly dark twelve-year-old wearing expensive sneakers, headphones, and a big thick jacket. He was carrying a rucksack and was holding a younger girl's hand firmly in his. She was dressed similarly in pink and purple and carried a small pink wheel-along trolley with a unicorn made on it. She also had shoulder-length hair that curled in at the bottom. Raqia smiled. The bowl cut every parent forced on their daughters till they turned into teenagers and rebelled.

The elder one saw their father and pointed and they both ran up. Varin looked thrilled to see them, beaming and hugging them and they hugged him back equally hard. Raqia was transported back to the days when her dad would return from weeks away and throw her into the air when she ran to greet him. "This is Anjanee and Anjali. My kids. And this is Professor Raqia Bareja. She's a scientist and works with the Army", he finally turned to bring her into the family group.

The younger one made a face as she touched her hair. "And you can guess my parents are movie buffs and grew up in the Nineties", she pouted. She had a strong accent but Raqia couldn't recognize it. "I refuse to be all chirpy because my name is Anjali. And I'm not helping my dad find a girlfriend. That's soo lame".

Her brother nudged her hard, " 'Shups Anj. No one asked you", he pointed out.

Their father was red in the face. "Girlfriend", he stammered. "Who asked you to find me a girlfriend?"

"Aaji did", the younger one immediately said. "She said if I'm named Anjali, I have a duty to the name. And she made Ma show me this old Hindi movie last hols. Kuch

Kuch Hota hai. Kuch Kuch hota hai, Rahul. Tum Nahi samjhoge", she mimicked as she tossed her head.

Raqia wanted to be in splits of laughter over Varin's obvious embarrassment and his daughter's antics, but she held it in somehow. The boy took a deep breath, indicated to his father that he was going to the conveyer belt, and stalked off, shaking his head.

She was left in the headlights. Anjali turned her acute attention to her. "Have you seen the movie", she demanded. Raqia had to nod her head. "Unfortunately, yes. I have seen it. More embarrassingly, I liked it. Didn't you?"

"No", the girl shook her head vehemently. "I didn't. It was all romantic and yucky. I love Studio Ghibli, Hunger Games, and Percy Jackson. Not this", she stretched out 'this', making her opinion very clear. "Have you seen Howl's, Moving Castle? It's not for children, you know."

"I know", Raqia said. "I've met Miyakazi. He spoke at my college after his film was shown and I was in the Student's Union so I escorted him and kept him company while he was waiting for the event to start".

Anjali looked at her with new respect before she turned to her father. "I like her", she announced pompously as she handed her bag to her father and then slipped her hand into her father's free hand. "I think she'll be good for the family".

The adults looked at each other flabbergasted. Anjali continued into the silence. "If Aaji marries your dad, will that make you, our aunt?"

"What", Varin exploded as he halted and looked at Raqia furiously. She looked back at him equally horrified before looking pointedly at the girl walking between them.

He controlled himself. "Who said that to you", he asked in a strained voice.

His daughter looked at him innocently. “Aaji did. She said we get to decide if we like him and if he’s grandfather material. And he was sitting next to her and laughing. He seemed nice”. Varin took a deep breath. His chest expanded. Raqia had to admire his physique. It looked like Batman’s. All molded and modeled. She noticed several other women enjoying the sight as well and felt a little flutter. ‘Mine’, was her first thought. ‘Go away.’ She must have glared at them because at least one visibly lowered her eyes and walked away quickly.

“I think you should go help your son”, Raqia said as softly as she could. “I’ll stay here with Anjali”.

Her gorilla shook his head and moved off without a word, even though his eyes promised that someone was going to pay for this, most probably her and the Major, if she was to hazard a guess. He went up to his son and spoke to him as he took his place at the conveyer belt. The boy looked around and took a deep breath. Once he’d decided there was nothing fun happening, he sauntered back to them.

“What did you say this time, squeak”, he asked his sister jovially. “Dad’s already looking tense”. “Oh, shut up Anna”, she told her brother calmly. Raqia noticed Anjali made a lot of announcements. She was going to be a good CEO one day. So far, she was thoroughly enjoying this. She wondered if she’d get along with the kid’s mother. ‘I mean, her morals sound like they’re compromised but the kids seem fun and confident’, she thought.

As if she read Raqia’s thoughts, Anjali turned and pronounced with complete confidence, “I’m going to be an actress”. “When you grow up”, Raqia added automatically. “No”, Anjali insisted firmly. “I’m going to be an actress like Ma. My stepfather is making a movie for me”.

Stunned, Raqia looked at Anjanee. He sighed and rolled his eyes before he said apologetically. "She is. Appa is a producer. That's a big part of why Aaji wanted us over. She wanted to be sure Anjali could handle it before it all got out of control. And Ma said Dada has to sign off. Which he won't do. He hates our stepdad. This week is going to be explosive. I'm sorry".

Raqia wanted to hug him hard. He sounded like he'd been a grown-up for the longest time. And was used to keeping the peace between his parents. She hadn't had to do that but she'd more or less raised herself and two younger brothers so she could sympathize with him wholeheartedly.

Varin came back with two bags. One was pink and the other was brown. They were both made with expensive leather.

"Shall we go", he asked.

Anjanee grabbed Anjali's smaller bag, and his sister's hand and they started towards the car parking.

"How's the football been", his father asked him.

"Good", the boy replied. "Away game next month. Coach says I can play forward."

"Dada, can we go for Italian please", the younger one said. "I'm hungry".

"Aaji's made Italian at home", her father said briskly. "And we need to call your mother to tell her you've reached safely".

"Okay dada", she said as she pulled out an iPhone from her pocket. Her father and brother grimaced and looked at each other. "Why", her father asked her. She shrugged her shoulders. "Appa said it's okay".

Varin sighed and took another deep breath. Raqia glared at the woman who swerved out of her path to come towards them. Varin may not have seen, but his daughter was watching her with a sly smile on her face when she looked down at her.

"Dada...", she started. Raqia glared at her. Anjali stuck out her tongue at her and laughed. It was a childish laugh. Her brother put an arm around her. "Anjali is dramatic. But pretty nice. Not mean or anything. Do you watch cricket", he asked? "Dada says you're with the Army and were teaching in Dehradun. What do you teach? I want to be a pilot when I grow up. In the air force".

"I teach medieval warfare and middle eastern politics", Raqia explained. "And I realized Anjali is nice. So are you. No, I don't watch cricket. I used to play basketball when I was a kid. I haven't played in a while. I do parkour and karate and ride horses though".

"Woah! Can you teach me parkour? Do you have kids", he asked?

"I'm not married", Raqia explained.

"She's very intelligent", their father said. "She studied at Oxford".

"I want to study there", Anjali said immediately.

"I thought you wanted to become an actress", her father teased.

She sighed impatiently. "I can be both. I'm only eight", she explained patiently. "I need to be eighteen before I can go to Oxford".

Raqia had a flashback to being twenty-five and having to come back from Oxford because her grandmother had died and her brothers were alone with her elderly grandfather. She had another flashback to being fourteen and saying goodbye to her dad. She'd missed him. Probably as much as these kids missed their dad. She still missed him even though he was back. She was just so angry at him that she didn't know how to voice it.

"I think I'll head back home now", she stammered. Varin looked at her confused. "Aren't you coming with us? I'm pretty sure your family would already have left for our place". His eyes narrowed – she couldn't tell if it was in mock or real anger. "I need to talk to my mother about being indiscreet in front of the kids".

Raqia shrugged. "I'll come a little later. I want to make some calls". This wasn't a lie. She wanted some time to herself. Dehradun had been lovely but it had felt too sensory. She wanted some time to herself away from people. Away from Varin.

"Look, I'll call you in a couple of hours. Do you need me to pick you up for dinner?"

"No", she must have sounded horrified because he drew back as if he'd been stung. "I mean", she stammered, "I'll come...with Abhay if he's free or I'll catch an Uber", she said hurriedly.

"If you're sure". He sounded disappointed. He suddenly bellowed at his kids in the back seat. "What does everyone want to eat for dinner? So that I can ask our guests as well".

"You cook, dada". His son said immediately. "No one cooks as well as you".

"Do you want to eat proper spicy Konkan style curry", Varin asked her. "I'm not fond of spicy food", Raqia confessed. She didn't know what to do, but somehow every sentence was driving them further apart. But it was hard to explain to someone with their children in the car that she'd developed stomach ulcers when she was younger from the stress and she couldn't eat spices...or deal with too much stress. 'Another reason I can't be an army wife', she thought to herself. 'First, my father went missing. If my husband goes missing on me...", she didn't want to complete the thought. She deliberately turned her thoughts to Oxford's spires. They were safer, even though right now they looked a little misty.

"Okay", Varin sounded like he was at a loss. "I'll make dal chawal as well. Is that what you want to eat?"

She shrugged. The car had stopped and she stepped out. It was the first time she'd stepped out like a queen, leaving him looking frazzled. Thanks to the kids. She decided she liked them very much. They waved to her from the car and she waved back as they left her sight.

Varin was correct. Her father and Mayank were already at Sanjana's and there was no food in the fridge. She had to order a pizza and then chew her way through it alone as she sat on her computer randomly surfing sites.

Remembering the emails she'd forwarded, she looked at her second email box but there was nothing there. The computer was just painfully slow. Frustrated, she set up a search to see what had been downloaded in the past month that was clogging it up. With two boys in the house, there was often some game or some illegally downloaded movie with their many viruses. She'd told them often to stop downloading and then in frustration, she'd bought the best antivirus, but it still wasn't enough.

There was some big program in the search that she didn't recognize but which had been deleted. It was a .exe file and it hadn't been fully deleted. Some of it had rolled back and the half-deleted files were still messing with the system. Rolling her eyes, she looked in the drawer for the external hard drive. If a virus had entered the system, she had better take a backup.

She had nothing to do while the antivirus was checking the system. It was going to take at least an hour. Then she'd have to take a backup of the computer. There was no way she could work for the rest of the evening but she couldn't leave the house either.

'I should do the dusting', she thought virtuously as she got up and found the duster. She did the drawing-room first, including watering the plants but her attention was on the only bedroom with its door closed – the Colonels. 'If I'm dusting, I should dust the Colonel's room', she told herself. 'We've all been away for a week. The rooms have been locked. It must look awful. And it's not like the maid doesn't go in there. I'm just going to look around. Just look, nothing else.'

She entered. It felt wrong just opening the door and crossing the threshold but she did it anyway.

She dusted very slowly, including looking inside the drawers but there was nothing out of the ordinary.

A memory hit her. Her father used to have a special place for his money when she was young. The back pocket of his dress pants. She'd have to check the pockets before the pants went for washing because he would invariably forget and then phone her from work to check before the pants went for laundry.

She opened his cupboard and looked through his trousers. There were only six so it wasn't a huge task. She struck gold on the third pair. Something bulky in the back pocket. 'Bingo', she thought as she reached in. There was a USB she didn't recognize in her hand. She stared at it. 'Should I check it now? If it's just songs Sanjana's given him, I'll feel stupid.'

Her phone rang suddenly. She looked at it. Of course, it was Varin. She did not want to spend time with the overload of cuteness that was his family right now. "Sorry, got a stomach ache. Going to bed", she texted. Somehow, she didn't want to do anymore dusting.

It was barely seven but at least the antivirus had finished its job. She started looking for jobs and MA applications. It was frustrating. She still had a year of MA to complete despite her age. No one wanted an expert on the Middle East if she didn't have a Ph.D. In desperation, she turned back to her emails to write to her tutor at Oxford. Maybe she could still get another scholarship and complete her MA. Her search showed her last mail to him was in the deleted folder. Frustrated with her computer, she shut it and went to bed.

She woke up in the middle of the night to see her phone blinking. There were six missed calls from Varin. She made a sudden decision. "Found a virus on the computer and a USB in the Major's room. Going to check it at work tomorrow", she texted before she fell asleep.

# CHAPTER SEVEN

The next morning. DD was waiting for her in the office with Varin Paranjape and another officer. Both were in battle fatigues which were slightly unexpected at eight on a Monday morning. Until the moment she saw them, Raqia had been exhausted. When she saw him again, her heart started racing and her tiredness disappeared. She could barely concentrate on what DD was saying.

"We need to monitor your home computer and laptop and their logging in and out times. A virus could have been uploaded via your home computer if you checked your work emails on that", DD announced. "Don't worry", she said more gently. "It's just a precaution".

"But information is getting out", Varin countered. "Over the past few months, description of our arms and ammunition made it across. Pakistanis are making exact replicas". "Or so our spies tell us", the other officer added laconically. Varin carried on without comment. "More importantly, I'm afraid that someone will hack our information systems and send wrong information to troops. I'm pretty sure the website hacking was to send a public signal that someone had gained access to the system. Everyone now knows that it's possible and probably available to the highest bidder. Can you imagine what will happen during a battle if the information systems crash or wrong information is sent to battalions? It'll be mayhem.

Worse, it'll be a slaughter. We know Major Singh was left in Pakistan by RAW, and Ms. Bareja has confirmed that he is her father, but what if he turned into a double agent while he was there?"

"I'm not sure he knows much about computers", Raqia said cautiously. 'I'd known the shit was going to hit the fan when I got back, but I hadn't realized how much,' she thought. 'Am I supposed to throw him under the bus? Or has he already thrown me?'

'There goes the pension', her second voice groaned. 'The extra income had been nice'.

'The first thing we need to check for is malware on your laptop", the second officer chimed in. "We've caught some malware on the system and even though we keep deleting them, more keep appearing. Seems to be a self-replicating virus but we need to check if they're entering the system from your laptop? That's pretty easy to check because luckily you haven't logged onto the system in the past few days". 'Thanks to someone here who kept me constantly busy,' she shot a scathing look at Varin who was conveniently studying the roof. There was a suspicious redness to his cheeks. 'Just wait till I get you alone, Varin Paranjape', she thought to herself. 'What do you plan to do with him exactly when you get him alone, her second thoughts asked. 'How long do you plan to yell at him and how long will you....'

For once, her third thoughts intervened. 'This is not a joke. You could have ended up going to jail as an accessory if you hadn't called him that night. You could still go to jail. You're on very thin ice".

"Okay, what else do you need me to do", she shrugged off her coat and put down her laptop on the table. "I want to...no, I need to prove I'm innocent. So, tell me what to do? Do I need to go through information systems to see if anything doesn't add up? Do I need to set up a camera near the home computer? Do we wiretap my phone?" The two officers straightened up. "Not bad suggestions", DD said with a grim look. "And I can ask the rest of your teams in the NSG to do the same till we know where the leak came from. But right now, perhaps the laptop".

"Oh, one thing", Raqia said, conscious that Varin hadn't mentioned it yet. "I found a strange USB in the house. Probably nothing, but I still brought it in. It's in my laptop bag".

"Okay", the second officer said. "What's on it?"

"No idea. I haven't watched it", Raqia said. "I...had a stomach-ache and went to sleep early". 'And woke up to six missed calls from the Colonel', she decided not to add.

"Let's check it now", Varin said. "Checking information systems is of course above Ms. Bareja's pay grade but it's what I'm paid to do, so I'll be doing that for a while, I guess".

Raqia found and handed the second officer the USB. She noticed he hadn't shared his name but Varin seemed to be listening to him.

"What the hell is this", he said as he played it on a standalone computer DD found them. "It's some kind of malware. Probably the kind that steals information from a system once it's installed. Probably works in tandem with the virus. Well done, you two", he looked at Varin and Raqia. "You've managed to get a huge part of the puzzle solved. I would say", he looked at Raqia, "that your father knows computers. Unless, and this seems unlikely, one of your brothers is a double agent, or someone broke in...No? Then let's bring him in. Varin, are you going to pick him up?"

Raqia could do nothing but twiddle her thumbs as they waited for word from Varin and his team. It finally came. The Second Officer's radio crackled. "We're in position", Varin reported.

"He's not answering the phone", Raqia said as she tried to call the house landline.

"Where's Mayank and Abhay? House looks empty. Sub missing." Varin reported.

"Hold on. I'm calling the boys", Raqia said anxiously. "Abhay, where are you? Major is the NSG hacker", she said quickly.

"Holy shit. I'm at school. Left home early. Mayank was home when I left. Is he okay", Abhay said quickly?

"Okay. I'll call him", she said quickly before cutting the call. Mayank answered on the eighth ring. "Driving, Di", he said quickly.

"Where's the Major", she asked anxiously.

"I left him at Sanjana's".

"Fuck. He's a spy", she said anxiously. "Okay, let me tell Varin".

"I'm on my way back, Di. Bye".

"He's at Sanjana's...Varin's mums' house", she yelled aloud. "This is too personal for him. Can we take a second team?"

"Fine", the second officer said.

"I'm going as well", Raqia said aggressively.

"Why", the officer argued. "You'll just be in the way".

"Doesn't matter. I'm going. His kids are there. That's my dad".

He studied her for a minute before he finally nodded his head.

It took everything for her to sit still while a second troop was dispatched and a Kevlar vest was procured for her. It was no use giving her a gun, and she said so. She hadn't had shooting practice in years. It would be more dangerous than helpful.

She held onto the roof of the rider's cabin of the black swat van. When they reached Hauz Khas, they had to depend on Varin for directions. She'd never been to the house. His voice on the radio sounded more and more robotic and she had to hold herself back from saying encouraging words to him. He wasn't in danger but his family was, and this hurt her. She'd liked the kids and Sanjana had become like a favorite aunt with her constant positivity.

They drew into position and everyone got out of the van. She found herself being led to where Varin was crouching.

"He's there", he said bleakly.

The house was on a small side street opposite a park. There was a long garden and the house was at the other end. They were lucky. The garden was very overgrown – Sanjana hadn't been exaggerating. The dining room faced the side and there was a window that allowed them to look in from the corner of the street with binoculars. And the Major was directly in their sights. He was laughing, which Raqia had never seen him do.

Anjali came into view. She had a book that she lifted and a shaft went through Raqia's heart. He was reading '*Where The Wild Things Are*'. She could see him mouthing words and she quoted them out aloud alongside.

"There should be a place where only the things you want to happen happen", he said as Anjali kept the book on the table between them and he showed the pictures to the little girl. There was a pile of books on the table. Many of them were hers'. She could make out the dog ears. He'd brought them down from Dehradun without telling her and somewhere between yesterday and today, he had brought over a large part of her childhood and was sharing it with other children. Her heart broke a little bit more. 'Does he have other children in Pakistan', she wondered? 'Did they get the father we didn't?'

Sanjana appeared behind them, laughing as she walked through an open door, presumably to the kitchen.

Her heart bled for the normality and happiness in front of her. The whiff of childhood and the childhood that was stolen from her. Maybe her father had also wanted a normal life and family but it had been stolen from him by his work. Maybe he'd missed them as much as they'd missed him. Her mind's eye showed her an imagined past where he'd never gone missing and they'd all been as happy as the scene in front of her.

"Should we shoot, sir; or do you want to interrogate him", a prosaic voice said near her through Varin's radio.

"You'll hit my daughter if you shoot at this range", Varin said savagely into the radio. "And we need him alive. Hold off".

"I'm going in", Raqia said impulsively.

"No, you're not. You're a civilian", Varin rumbled above her.

"I'm a civilian who knows the aggressor, the victim as well as karate and parkour. No one else has all that here. Stop thinking with your heart, Varin", Raqia said in a low voice; not wanting both teams to hear her plead. "And you're here. Shoot him the moment I get him away from your family".

"She's right", the second officer spoke in his laconic tone through the phone. "Do you need a direct order from me?"

"No sir", Varin said woodenly. "Sending her in now. Can we pretend she's an honorary captain so that her family will get a pension this time?"

"If she gets him or gets killed trying Colonel, she'll get a bigger payout for being a civilian", the laconic voice came over the phone. "Send her in now, Colonel". His patience was at an end.

Varin pressed a gun into her hand. "Here's a gun. Don't use it if you can help it. That's my kids in there. And my mother. Christ, I was worried about custody this morning. I can't even keep them alive in Delhi".

Raqia accepted the gun and put it into the back of her trousers. She walked through the front gate of the house, calling out for Sanjana.

The Major looked up and smiled before he looked puzzled. "Hi, beta. Don't you have work today", he asked. "Why are you looking for Sanjana"?

Sanjana came out of the kitchen just then. "Hey Raqia", she called out. "Aren't you at work? I was just making lunch with Anjanee. Join us".

Anjali came rushing up. "I got new books", she said happily as she grabbed Raqia's hand. "You weren't here for dinner. We had fun. Dada cooked chicken pasta because Aaji doesn't like spices. And we met your brother. He's funny. And your other brother took us to this bookshop nearby. The owner looks at everyone and decides what books they should read. But your dad brought us some books. He insisted on '*Where The Wild Things Are*' because it was your favorite. It's cute. Not Miyakazi of course". She chattered as she led Raqia inside.

Her father looked at her in bewilderment as she stopped in front of him. "Why are you here", he said. His eyes fell on her vest and he half rose from the chair. "Why are you in a bulletproof vest?"

"Dad", Raqia asked, her voice hoarse. "The army needs to ask you a few more questions. Would you come with me please"?

"What's this about", Sanjana asked, looking alarmed, as the Major said, "No".

The next thing they knew was that he'd pulled a gun from his waistband and grabbed Anjali, even though Raqia tried to hold onto her. His eyes were no longer puzzled now. They just looked bleak and angry. He no longer looked like the same man. Lines appeared on the sides of his face that made him look older and harder. "I didn't survive all those years in jail on the other side to go to jail on this side, my dear. I have nothing to live for, really, except for the money. I'll take all of you with me. Why should I have all the fun?"

Sanjana and Anjali both screamed but Anjali was choked off almost immediately by the Major's arm around her throat. As Anjali started making choking sounds, Anjanee came running from the kitchen. He yelled as he saw his sister being choked to death but stopped in his tracks as the Major waved his gun in his and Sanjana's direction. "I have four hostages. I can kill one easy and still have the rest of you", he said harshly. "Get back".

"Oh dad, why did you do it", Raqia asked sorrowfully.

"Because I had no choice", her father snarled. "RAW left me and the Pakis put me in jail. Since I didn't have papers on me, they didn't have to declare me. I wasn't a prisoner of war, just an ordinary Pakistani citizen. Who cares about one of those? I was in jail for sixteen years. When you caught their attention, they trained and sent me here. I was not only to conduct espionage but also to open up the NSG information services. I was a bomb. No, I was a ticking nuclear bomb. I could do more damage for them than a thousand attacks on Mumbai".

"But you didn't study the most important thing", Raqia said sorrowfully. It felt like a weight on her chest. 'Like you're lighting your father's pyre', her inner voice said sorrowfully. "You didn't study me". She was well within arms grasp of him. It was easy. With one arm movement, she twisted the arm in which he held his weapon upwards, and then put a little more weight till she heard the arm crack and the screaming start. "You didn't realize that I'm a black belt in Karate". She swept out a leg and spun, trying to take his leg out from under him. But he was an army man as well. He scrambled out of the way and fired at her. The bullet went wild but Sanjana and Anjali screamed. Through her earpiece, she could hear Varin calmly telling the soldiers to get into place. 'No', she yelled. 'That's too dangerous.

The Major grabbed Anjali with his uninjured arm while trying to hold the gun. By now, Raqia was prowling around him, trying to distract him. He turned, yelling at her to stop. Or he would shoot the kid. She stopped and launched herself at the table. With a leap, she climbed onto it and started throwing things at him. As he dealt with the sudden missiles, she leaped. This time, she body-slammed straight into him taking him down. "Anjali, get to your brother", she yelled. As the little girl tried to run, the major caught her leg and pulled her back, kicking and screaming. He wasn't going to let his hostage go. But it was too late. Raqia was too close. She raised her arm and aimed a karate punch at his knee. He lay screaming to the floor, his knee shattered and his leg at an awkward angle. She rose gracefully and pulled Anjali far out of the Major's grasp and held her trembling body against her own as she looked down in sorrow at her screaming father. "His mother called him wild thing and Max said I'll eat you up so he was sent to bed without eating anything", she quoted softly. "He became king of the beasts and the wild rumpus".

"We've got it", Varin said from behind her as his team entered the room.

Feeling bile in her mouth and knowing she was going to throw up, Raqia rushed into the garden and threw up into one of the bushes. A hand rubbed her back soothingly. She flinched. "It's me, Di", Abhay said in a soft voice. "It's just me". She turned and hid her face in his shoulder as he held her tightly.

"Thank you", Varin said coldly behind her. "But I still need to figure out if he was working alone or if there was a team. And if there was more damage done to the systems. This hasn't ended. Do you want to help me question him?".

"Give me some time to process", Raqia snapped at him from Abhay's arms, responding to his tone. "I can deal with one fear at a time. I just maimed my father and put him into jail - after your army took away twenty-three years of his life; and cleared him. This is not about a job. This is about people's lives. I don't know what you want. I'll happily give up the job if it means getting my father and my life back. I don't want this, do you understand? You – me. I can't deal with this, and I don't want to. I want to leave all this behind and go back to my studies. I don't want to worry about you and your bloody traitor, do you understand. I don't want to be stuck in limbo like I have been for twenty-three years, left dealing with kids and bills and waiting for you to come back. Killing my dreams to cook dinner every night".

The kids and Sanjana stood behind him with their eyes bulging. Raqia couldn't handle it. She turned and buried her face in Abhay's shoulder as he folded her protectively into a hard hug.

"You're right. I wouldn't be able to handle the thought of Anjali going through what you've been through. And Anjanee is just a couple of years younger than you were then. You are and have always been very brave", Varin said softly. "And thank you for saving my family".

"Perhaps the children should go inside", Sanjana said at the same moment just as quietly.

Raqia stole a look at Varin, not sure what she was hoping for from him, but he'd already turned away. "I'll take the Major in and get him to speak about his connections", Varin continued woodenly. "I'll take the team away now. I presume you'll be taking some time off to deal with everything. And my boss plans to recommend you for a pretty big award. Your money worries are over. You can go back to your precious Oxford".

He walked into the house. Raqia could hear him gathering the kids into his arms and praising them for being so brave that he had to take the Major in, but would leave a guard outside the house. He came out and without looking at her, saluted and got into his car. The next thing she knew, he was gone. Sanjana ran out. "Huh", she said in exasperation. "What is wrong with that man", she exclaimed.

"Perhaps we should go", Abhay said awkwardly. "I know you must be shaken and we're so sorry. But I think Di needs some time to get over this mess".

"But are you in any condition to go home?" Sanjana exclaimed. "I understand that Raqia needs some time to heal but you'll be all alone. Stay. The youngsters also need time to process everything that's happened today. You all can huddle together and I'll cook....or order in. I'd love some help to take care of the kids. Stay for a week. Stay here", she said wildly.

"No, thanks", Raqia looked up to say. "I want some time to process today".

Anjali walked out of the house and came straight to Raqia. "I've decided I'm going to Oxford", she said as she looked up through her bangs at her; her big eyes solemn. "I don't want to be stuck here in this country".

Raqia had to laugh as she reached down and hugged the girl who hugged her back readily. "Can I come and visit you in Oxford", the little girl whispered in her ear. "Dada looked unhappy when he left so I don't know when I'll see you next. Can I take your number from Aayi"?

"Of course", Raqia exclaimed. "Let me say goodbye to your brother."

She went into the kitchen where Anjanee was packing chilas like a robot. He looked up and down again. "Thank you", he mumbled softly. She waited but he refused to look at her. "Goodbye Anjanee. It was nice to meet you", she said finally. "Bye", he mumbled, avoiding her face. Tears started rolling down her face and she didn't know what to do. She stood there for another minute till he finally turned his big soft eyes at her. "Dada was unhappy that you didn't come yesterday. But thank you for saving us today", he said quietly as he thrust the packet of chilas into her hand. She had no answer.

The two of them limped to the road where they found Varin had left an official vehicle for them. Abhay pulled out his phone as they got in. It was still ringing. "Yes Mayank", he said. "Di and I are headed home. Di got the Major. He turned out to be a spy after all."

# CHAPTER EIGHT

Raqia didn't see Varin all month. If he came over to the office, he made a point of not being around during the time she was there. Other people came to take her statement. DD offered her leave and counseling and she accepted both but they ended. She even tried to walk into his office to be told that he was out of town. His boss, the officer who had refused to offer his name, was there, and he winked at her before he went back to work. He was wearing his uniform and Raqia was shocked to see that he was a Brigadier. This war between countries wasn't going to end, she knew. There would be more sacrifices.

Since it was the weekend, she decided to go back to Dehradun. It made more sense than hanging around Delhi where she might run into Varin, even if only in her fantasies.

She must have looked sad that evening because Mayank knocked on her door at night. "I picked up a copy of '*Where The Wild Things Are*' from the bookshop", Mayank said shyly. "In case you want to read it together".

"I want to hear it too", Abhay pouted from his doorway, where he must have heard the knock. "I missed out on it. Dad only read Chacha Choudary and Phantom to us".

"Can he", their youngest brother asked sweetly? "I mean, today's for you, Raqia. I haven't got a chance to speak with you in the longest time, but Abhay wants to be here too". She sighed and nodded. The only plan she'd had so far for the evening was to stare at her phone and cry a little.

Her brothers got into the bed on both sides of her and pulled blankets over themselves so that she was sandwiched between them. Raqia put her head on Mayank's shoulder and they opened the first page. "That night Max wore his wolf suit and made mischief of one kind", her brother read out before turning the page. "And another. His mother called him "wild thing". "I'll eat you up" so he was sent to bed without eating anything. That very night in Max's room a forest grew".

By this time Raqia was sobbing. Mayank carried on to the end of the very short book.

Raqia sobbed harder through the story till she was gulping in breaths like a child by the end of it.

He gently ran his hand down her head. "It's okay, Di. It's okay to play with wild things. Inside all of us is hope. Inside all of us is fear. Inside all of us is an adventure. Inside all of us is a wild thing", he quoted softly. "But that warm supper waiting for us in our room is so important as well. Dad stayed with the wild things and never came home but you came home and gave us that warm supper. You and Dad kept us together after Ma's death. Then you dealt with Dad's disappearance. We left too much on your shoulders. We've still put too much on your shoulders. You're right. You should go to Oxford to finish your studies. If you decide to give Varin Paranjape a chance, then maybe you'll have him making you that warm dinner as long as he can. But Abhay and I and Sanjana will help raise the children. Don't they say, it takes a village to raise a child?

If you decide not to spend your life with him, we'll understand as well", Abhay added. "After all, you shouldn't resent your husband and children as well as your siblings".

"But you need to step out of your comfort zone and make a decision. Do something", Mayank said firmly.

"He won't talk to me", Raqia wailed. "And I liked Anjanee. He was so brave. And Anjali took my number in secret and I speak with her every night. I read her this book and 'Wrinkle in Time' and we discussed Sednik and Frances Hodgson Burnett and Madeleine L'Engle and Amrita Pritam an hour ago".

Her brother laughed. "Okay then. But do you want to make an honest man of him? I'll understand if you don't want to and prefer to keep it dishonest".

She nodded as water ran out of her nose. "He won't speak to me", she wailed again as she wiped her nose on her sleeve.

"He'll talk to you in Rishikesh ", Abhay declared.

"He won't", she wailed further. "I went to his office to see him and he wasn't there. I even went to his Gym, and those are the two places he never misses".

"Of course he will speak with you", Mayank said in a no-nonsense tone as Abhay handed her a tissue and then hugged her so hard that her hand couldn't reach her nose. "Hadn't you promised to listen to me? I give the best advice, you said".

# CHAPTER NINE

It was barely four on March 11th when Raqia woke the boys up, but since she hadn't slept all night, she felt entitled. Unfortunately, by the time they left Dehradun, it had already started to rain. They went straight to Ram Jhula and parked their car so that they could walk. By the time they finished their preparations, the beach was already so crowded that they took twenty minutes to walk down the riverfront to the yoga ashram Sanjana, Varin, and the kids were staying at. The rain made everything muddy but the sun was peeking through the clouds.

There was a huge stage set up on the opposite side in front of the Shiv statue and there was already someone giving a yoga demonstration that was being broadcast for everyone within twenty kilometers to hear. The Shiv statue was still the central point of the area but it seemed lost amongst the crowds of humanity.

"Maybe going up to the Neelkanth Mahadev temple today is not a great idea", Raqia said as she lost her nerve. "It's going to be filthy".

"And crowded", Mayank said grimly. He took a deep breath and exhaled loudly. "Oh well. Anything for love". She punched him hard on the shoulder and he dodged and giggled.

"Here", Sanjana waved from the upper balcony of one of the buildings. She was dressed in a skimpy camisole and yoga pants and was glowing. “Up here. There are stairs to the side”.

They ran to the entrance to find Anjanee waiting for them, looking taller and browner than he’d been in Delhi.

“I’m so hungry,” he groaned as soon as he saw them. “Did you bring chips? Don’t tell Aayi. She keeps wanting us to be healthy. Although”, he brightened. “She knows the best places for sweets and cakes”.

They walked in and up the stairs to the beautiful balcony Sanjana waiting for them. After they’d all hugged, they sat down to have fruit and coffee. “Anjali’s delaying him,” Sanjana said. “They’ve gone for a walk”.

Varin and Anjali arrived not long after. While Anjali ran up to hug them, he just looked stunned to see them all and then resigned. “Darling”, his mother called out. “I’m keeping your coffee warm”.

“Thanks. It’s pretty cold today”, he said as he came closer and took off his wet jacket. “So, what’s the plan?”

“Well, Neelkanth Mahadev temple, then lunch and the Arati in the evening followed by dinner. And then the midnight raves for me and Mayank and Abhay”, his mother giggled. “This place is really fun around this time”.

“It’s a romantic place, isn’t it”, Mayank said sweetly as he leaned towards Sanjana. “They say you’ll get married if you go to the Mahadev Temple today. I don’t know about you all, but I want to get married.”

Varin blinked and finally laughed wryly, “I’ll take my chances. But we should leave now. The path is very treacherous. And the crowds will be horrific. I’m not sure why you want to do this today, Ma”.

“Because it’s important, Varin”, his mother replied pertly. “Let’s go”.

He still hadn’t said a word or looked at Raqia.

It was a trek back to their cars through the crowds. Luckily, he'd brought a driver but it took a good half hour just to drive to the car park. By the time they had sorted themselves out, Sanjana, Varin, Anjali, and Raqia were in his car and the boys and driver were in theirs.

It was a difficult drive and Anjali kept them entertained. Varin focussed on the steep winding slippery road. Raqia focused on the back of his head.

The temple was crowded, muddy, and humid and somehow, they got divided at the entrance. Sanjana, Anjali, and Raqia found themselves on one side with the men all in the other line. But Raqia found herself facing Varin as she poured her prasad over the idol. His eyes were closed and he was frowning but at least he was here in front of her. She said a quick prayer.

"I hope you're praying that we make it down without getting too filthy", Sanjana whispered. "This is really Parvati's penance".

"Hahaha", Raqia whispered back. "She did her meditations for a thousand years to marry him. I'm planning to do it for one day and one day only".

"Good luck, girl", Sanjana whispered back. "He's worth it".

They made their way down, stopping for momos and pakoras on the way. It took them so long to make it past the lines of cars coming up the mountain that it was almost five by the time they hit the town.

"Arati and then dinner and bed", Varin said dryly as he finally turned his car into the Ram Jhula parking. "And I'll happily skip the arati for the midnight bhajans".

"Noo", Anjali protested. "We have to attend the arati. Especially in front of the Shiva statue. I promised to record it for the kids in my class so that they can see what it's like here. They've never seen a North Indian MahaShivratri. It's so crazy up here. I mean, they've been going wild over the evening arati at the ghats, but the crowds right now are just gigantic".

"Ma", Varin protested and then shut up when his daughter turned a baleful eye on him.

It was sunset by the time they parked inside the ashram gate and got one of the last ferryboats across. Varin had not said a word to Raqia all day. Foreigners were taking photos all around them while she sat in determined silence, hoping against hope that she'd win him back. She wasn't named for Parvati for nothing.

The arati had started by the time they made their way into the Parmarth Niketan Ashram's gates. Despite the unending drizzle, the place was already packed with visitors facing the giant Shiv statue and swaying to the high and low-pitched voices of the young and old singers' as they melded together harmoniously. Raqia's eyes, like everyone around her, went immediately to the gigantic marble statue sitting serenely in the Ganga.

Anjali brought out her iPhone and started live-streaming the arati while Anjanee and Sanjana steered her around in a circle to film the full spectacle. And a spectacle it was. There were dozens of singers sitting on one side, while hundreds of people streamed in and magically found space to sit under the covered podium behind the singers or on the covered stage at a distance that was used for yoga in the mornings. Only a few hardy souls stood in the rain in front of the Statue including Varin. Raqia couldn't take her eyes off him. Her grumpy Varin outlined against the white statue above him was a breath-taking sight, especially in the rain. the muscles in his shoulders and thighs were outlined by the wet clothes that clung to him.

As the sky darkened, more and more people streamed through the gates, till the only places not filled with humans were the pits that were kept ready for havans and a big covered box behind the havan pit. The bhajan's stopped and the pundit began swinging the large diya to the rhythmic sounds of the huge crowd bellowing out the arati. The Moon rose behind the statue, making it look even whiter and more mysterious.

The arati continued, this time with people coming forward to swing the Diya. "Come on", Anjali said impatiently as she got up and fought through the crowds to stand beside Varin and Anjanee. The rest of them followed but by the time they got to the front, it was full; and they found themselves standing a few rows behind Varin, although Raqia could still see his broad shoulders above the crowd.

When the Diya came to Raqia, she took it gingerly. It had multiple lights on it which together created almost a small inferno. 'Please help me, Shivji', she prayed to the statue as she swung the Diya. There was no sign from the huge statue. She sighed. 'I wonder if Parvati ever wondered what she'll do if Shiv didn't open his eyes for her', she thought. 'Or was she so determined that she was ready to wait for another thousand years?' Mayank nudged her shoulder and she handed the Diya over reluctantly. "Shivji, please complete our family". Mayank said, just loud enough for her to hear. "Your family was created in unusual circumstances as well, and it's known as the greatest love story in the world. You were always your wife's biggest support; as she was yours. She helped you survive the poison and you loved her so much through every incarnation and avatar of hers that you've always been her guard.

Suddenly, a flock of parrots flew past the statue. Sanjana frowned. “Parrots”, she queried loudly enough for them to hear. “Isn’t it rather late for birds to be flying around? I thought birds went to sleep at night”.

“They’re an omen, Aaji”, Anjali said confidently. “Parrots are associated with Goddess Meenakshi. And she’s a form of Parvati. The loving form. And the God of love as well. I don’t remember his name but the one who shoots arrows like Cupid”. The parrots, obviously displeased by the incredible noise of the arati, squawked so loudly as they flew past that they momentarily drowned out the sound of the singers.

Raqia looked down and smiled shyly. She’d asked for a sign and Parvati had replied, even if Shiv had not. Too late now. She was committed to what she needed to do tonight.

The crowds slowly dispersed as the arati got over but Viran didn’t move. He stayed where he was, staring at the huge white statue as if he was mesmerized.

The pundit and his disciples lit the fire in the havan pit despite the drizzle and started reciting their prayers loudly. “Children, Varin”, Sanjana called loudly and Varin reluctantly turned around to face the havan; his hands stuffed into his pockets. Anjali was already filming the havan with Abhay holding an umbrella over her so that her camera didn’t get wet.

Raqia looked up once and said a quick prayer to the huge white Shiv sitting in meditation with his eyes closed above her. Her heart filled with love for the unshaven, surly man standing in front of her. She felt hot and mushy inside, as well as protective. She’d never felt like this before. It was a new feeling.

‘Time to make a fool of myself, she decided. ‘Shivji, help, please. Parvatima, you know I’m doing the right thing. Now make him love me'. As if in answer, there was an audible splash as river water hit the last stair. Somewhere far away there was a roar which if you listened carefully, was getting louder.

This was her chance. Abhay handed her the box and she slipped to one knee in front of the fire. The pundit must have seen a lot because he barely glanced at Raqia as he continued his litany. But the apprentices stammered and stalled, as they gazed at her in confusion. People turned to see why the apprentices were no longer reciting the prayers and nudged each other as they saw Raqia down on one knee with a jewelry box in her hand. Anjali, who'd already taken up the best vantage point to the right of them, started giving a live update of everything going on. Sanjana turned on her camera as well, while someone in the background screamed and called her friends.

Varin finally looked up from his contemplation of the fire and looked confused at the pandemonium. He looked at his mother and her phone before he realized everyone was staring at something in front of him. He frowned as he looked at Raqia on one knee.

The roar grew louder and they all instinctively looked up as a plane flew above the water. It was a single-seater which was why it could fly so low. Behind it was a banner that read "Marry me, Colonel". Anjali and Anjanee jumped, pointed, and screamed as the plane slowly flew past. Even Sanjana and the boys were grinning as they watched it fly past.

Varin watched the plane fly past in silence before he turned to look at Raqia who was still leaning on the ground.

"I thought the Major had made you decide never to get married. What's going on?"

"Colonel Varin Paranjape, I want to spend the rest of our lives together", Raqia recited. "For better or worse, in richness and poverty, in health and illness. For this life and the next. Would you make me the happiest woman in the world"?

People ran back to see what was going on as the plane slowly disappeared and news spread that it was connected to something at the ashram. Some looked at her in confusion. Folks further away asked each other what was happening. A few white folks who understood what Raqia was saying, cheered. Anjali was now yelling hysterically into her phone although Anajanee when she stole a peek at him, had a look of sadness on his face. It broke Raqia's heart. She'd been there. Unable to trust any elder.

"What about the kids", Varin asked suspiciously. "And the Ph.D.?"

"They'll have a village to raise them", Mayank said huskily.

"And if...when I have to go to the border"?

"Life doesn't come with guarantees. But living with love for a few days is better than living a long life without it", Abhay said from the other side.

"Say yes, dada", Anjali yelled. "I want to go to Oxford".

He still didn't reply.

"You better say yes quickly", Raqia suddenly said frantically. "Because I'm going to slip. My knee has gone to sleep".

"Hahaha", Varin let out a laugh just as Raqia started slipping on the wet surface, tried to rise, yelled, and fell forward. Varin saw the ring slip from her grasp and jumped to grab it before it fell into the river. He ended up sprawled sideways and she found herself with her nose pressed on his thigh again. The crowd oohed.

Raqia let out a sigh as she burrowed her head in his leg rather than look at the crowd that was surely grinning. 'This is my life', she thought resignedly. 'This man can make me look ridiculous in any circumstances. I could bring down a double agent but I'm sprawled on a wet platform in Rishikesh on Shivratri being recorded for posterity. This will be all over the internet tomorrow. Perhaps I can change my name to Sita and the earth will open up and swallow me right now.

"Perhaps you could get off my leg and stop grumbling to yourself", the man rumbled. "You do know you aren't actually thinking. You're talking to yourself. You're mouthing the words and right now, I can hear you bad-mouthing me. Not very romantic".

She buried her head more tightly against his leg until a laugh rumbled through him. "Incidentally, you may not be perfect, but I think my family likes you more than they like me, and I'm perfect. So, I guess I'll just have to keep you".

"What are they saying", they could hear Anjali ask in frustration. "He said yes", Sanjana whispered loudly. "Are they getting married tonight", Anjali asked. "Perhaps", Mayank said gaily. "It would be the perfect night. Because it's endless. But I'm looking forward to doing up the pandal as well".

They helped each other up. Their audience started clapping as they stood up.

"Stay with me always", Varin whispered to her. "I'll deal with all your wild things".

www.ingramcontent.com/pod-product-compliance
Lightning Source LLC
LaVergne TN
LVHW091114150826
845673LV00002B/816

* 9 7 9 8 8 8 6 6 7 4 5 3 8 *